Ja… a cold sweat. Fumbling for the light, he turned it on.

"Nightmare," he said to himself. "You didn't propose."

A message from his subconscious—that's what this nightmare had been about. Sarah had thrown him a curve tonight. He hadn't expected her to turn down his suggestion that they live together. Just as he hadn't expected her to insist on marriage.

Dreams were not to be taken literally—everyone knew that. His subconscious did not want him to propose. It wanted him to make a plan to deal with Sarah, and act on it. He could do that.

But his plan would not include a wedding ring.

Dear Reader,

Happy Valentine's Day! Your response to our FABULOUS FATHERS has been tremendous, so our very special valentine to you is the start of our SUPER FABULOUS FATHERS—larger-than-life super dads who make super husbands! And Barbara McMahon's *Sheik Daddy* is just that. Years ago, gorgeous Ben Shalik had loved Megan O'Sullivan with all his heart, then disappeared, leaving her with a baby girl he never knew existed. And now, the royal daddy was back.... Look for more SUPER FABULOUS FATHERS throughout the year.

To celebrate the most romantic day of the year all month long, we're proud to present VALENTINE BRIDES. Reader favorite, author Phyllis Halldorson starts off the series with *Mail Order Wife*, which is exactly what confirmed bachelor Jim Buckley finds waiting on his doorstep! Christine Scott's *Cinderella Bride* proves that fairy tales can come true when Cynthia Gilbert reluctantly says "I do" to a marriage of convenience. In *The Husband Hunt* by Linda Lewis, Sarah Brannan's after a groom, but the man she's in love with proposes to be something *entirely* different.

You won't want to miss our other VALENTINE BRIDES—*Make-Believe Mom* by Elizabeth Sites and *Going to the Chapel* by Alice Sharpe. Because when Cupid strikes—marriage is sure to follow!

Happy Reading!

Melissa Senate
Senior Editor

THE HUSBAND HUNT

Linda Lewis

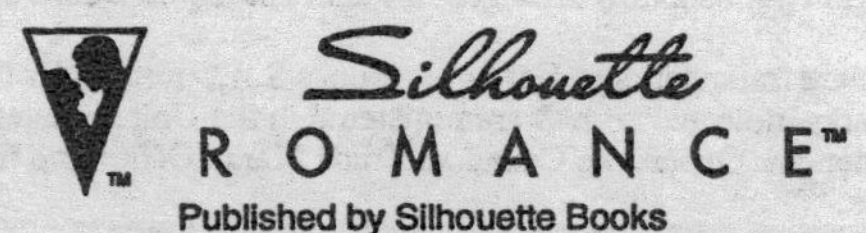

Published by Silhouette Books
America's Publisher of Contemporary Romance

For Lewis A. Grudzien and Mary Opal West, two special members of my personal version of the Brannan family.

ISBN 0-373-19135-9

THE HUSBAND HUNT

This edition published by arrangement with Harlequin Books S.A.

Printed in U.S.A.

Books by Linda Lewis

Silhouette Romance

Honeymoon Suite #1113
The Husband Hunt #1135

LINDA LEWIS

was born and raised in Texas. She lived in New York, Philadelphia and Chicago before settling down in New Orleans. Linda is an attorney and now resides with her family and an embarrassing number of dogs and cats.

Dear Reader,

February. Fifth-grade art class. Red construction paper, white paper doilies. Ribbons and lace and Elmer's glue. I worked and worked and came up with a veritable masterpiece of a valentine. On the fateful day, I shyly handed it to the boy of my dreams.

He gave his valentine to someone else. I was crushed, heartbroken. I never gave another valentine to a beau—at least not until he sent me one first.

Sarah Brannan, the heroine of *The Husband Hunt*, would never leave it to any mere male to decide on his own to send her a valentine—not if she really wanted the card (or the man).

Here's what she would do: Around the end of January Sarah would send him a calendar for February, with a lipstick heart drawn around the fourteenth. She'd follow up with daily valentines to him, signed "Your Secret Admirer."

If the man hadn't gotten the message by the tenth of February, she'd buy the valentine she'd picked out for him to send her. She'd put an *X* where his signature should go, then mail it to him, enclosing a self-addressed, stamped envelope. If the valentine came back signed, she'd know she'd gotten her man. If not, she still wouldn't give up.

There's always next year.

I hope you enjoy meeting Sarah. I wish I'd known her when I was in the fifth grade.

Happy Reading,

Linda Lewis

Chapter One

"*I love you, Sarah. Will you marry me?*"

Sarah Brannan sent the message mentally, then watched closely as the man sitting opposite her at the dining room table took another bite of chocolate meringue pie.

Jake Logan was not getting it.

With a tiny shrug, Sarah gave up on telepathy and went back to gazing dreamily at Jake. Had any man ever been so handsome? Dark brown hair, conservatively cut...gold-flecked brown eyes.... Resting her chin on her hand, she let her gaze drift down, past his sexy mouth and square jaw to his broad shoulders. The man was gorgeous. And he was going to be all hers. Delicious shivers ran up and down her spine at the thought.

Sarah sat up straight and chided herself for ogling. She wasn't so shallow that she'd fallen for a handsome face and a magnificent body. She was a Brannan woman, after all, and Brannan women had standards.

Jake Logan met every one of them. He was honest, hardworking, generous and kind. Intelligent and successful, too.

But she wasn't so smitten that she couldn't be objective. Jake Logan did have one fault. He was a man of few words. And he tended to use those words to ask questions or give orders. That was why he knew so much more about her background than she did about his.

When she'd started working for Jake, the strong attraction she'd felt to the quiet man with the golden eyes had made her nervous. Sarah talked when she was nervous. Incessantly. When Jake had begun venturing out of the executive suite to spend more and more time personally reviewing her work, she'd talked and talked. Mostly about her family. All she knew about Jake's family was that his parents had divorced when he was very young. He hadn't volunteered that information. She'd asked.

In his own laconic way Jake had gotten across his intentions for tonight, even though she'd had to read between the lines. Who wanted a smooth-talking man skilled in verbal foreplay, anyway? Not her. She didn't need words from Jake. All she needed was his love.

"The perfect end to a perfect meal." Jake leaned back in his chair, every inch of his six-foot-plus frame radiating well-fed satisfaction. He frowned when he looked at her untouched pie. "You didn't eat much. Do you feel all right?"

"I feel fine." Except for the butterflies doing somersaults in her stomach. She couldn't eat with that going on. No woman waiting for a marriage proposal would be calmly chewing and swallowing. Especially a woman who had waited. And waited. Lightly drumming her fingers on the linen tablecloth, Sarah gave Jake an encouraging smile.

Maybe she shouldn't have fixed such an elaborate dinner. Candlelight and four courses had seemed the right thing to do for such a momentous occasion. Now she wondered if she should have suggested McDonald's instead. A quick Big Mac and he'd be on his knees this very moment—not eyeing the pie as if he were thinking about seconds.

Sarah stood and whisked the pie plate off the table. "Coffee?" she asked as she walked from the dining alcove to the kitchen.

The way to a man's heart might be through his stomach, but Jake had eaten enough for one evening. For this evening, anyway. Before he'd left town yesterday he'd told her he had something important to discuss with her when he returned. Sarah had guessed right away that he was going to ask her to marry him. She'd known for weeks what her answer would be. But at the rate Jake was going, she'd be an old maid before she ever got the chance to say yes.

Sarah put a filter in the coffee maker and spooned in the coffee. A little more patience was all she needed. She would be saying yes any minute now. She grinned. Her family would be pleased. She wasn't going to be an old maid, after all. They thought she was well on the way to spinsterdom, and she really couldn't blame them. Brannan women married young.

Sarah's oldest sister, Barbara, had married Vince Hall the summer she turned eighteen, right after Vince graduated from Texas A&M. Laura, the middle sister, had been forced to wait until she was twenty-one. Colt McCauley, Laura's beau, wouldn't even talk about getting hitched until he quit the rodeo circuit and started law school.

Sarah was twenty-six years old and she had never been engaged. She hadn't even dated anyone seriously—except Rusty, and he hardly counted—until Jake. Not that she and Jake had dated, exactly. Dates meant dinners at restaurants, dancing, going to the movies. They hadn't gone out much. Granny Brannan would say they'd been keeping company. Sarah liked the sound of that.

She and Jake had mostly stayed in, at her apartment or his condominium, keeping each other company. They hadn't needed distractions or entertainment. More often than not, she had cooked dinner for the two of them. Cooking was the only feminine wile Sarah was willing to use to get her man—unlike her sisters, who'd used every female snare in the Brannan women's bag of tricks to get theirs.

Feeling smug and virtuous, Sarah took two mugs from the cupboard and filled them with freshly brewed coffee. The transition from courtship to marriage wouldn't be difficult. She and Jake were acting like a happily married couple already. Except for sex, of course. Jake hadn't tried to hustle her into bed at the first opportunity. That was both a blessing and a curse. She appreciated his gentlemanly restraint, but by now she was more than ready for him to propose.

She wouldn't object if he wanted to anticipate the wedding night, either. She'd been fantasizing about making love with him for weeks now. Virtue might be its own reward, but it was getting darn uncomfortable. Hopefully, Jake didn't believe in long engagements. Sarah filled the cream pitcher and dreamed of a Christmas wedding.

Jake appeared in the kitchen doorway just as Sarah had everything ready. Resting one shoulder against the doorframe, he said, "Coffee smells good. Let's have it on the patio."

Quickly, Sarah took a tray from the cabinet and arranged the mugs, cream pitcher and sugar bowl on it. The patio was perfect—the big Texas sky filled with stars, moonbeams dancing on the waters of Lake Austin. Sarah sighed happily. Jake had a romantic streak, after all. She had wondered about that. He was a great kisser, but—that little flaw, again—he wasn't verbally demonstrative. He'd never told her he loved her. But he would tonight.

Jake took the tray from her and led the way out the sliding glass door. He put the tray on the low table in front of the padded redwood love seat. When they were sitting side by side, he slid one arm around her shoulders and looked up at the moon.

"Nice night for late November, isn't it? I've been in Austin for more than ten years and I still haven't gotten used to the vagaries of Texas weather."

He must be nervous, too. Why else would he be talking about the weather? Jake never made small talk. Usually, she talked enough for both of them, but tonight her tongue seemed to be stuck to the roof of her mouth. Sarah leaned forward, splashed cream into the two mugs, handed one to Jake, then reached for the sugar bowl.

"Thanks. Sarah?"

She looked at him expectantly, her breath trapped in her chest. "Yes?" she squeaked.

"You've put four spoons of sugar in your coffee. Won't it be too sweet?"

Her breath came out in a whoosh. "No. I like it sweet." She took a sip and almost gagged.

Jake took the mug from her and dumped the contents into the flower bed. "I'll fix you another cup." He started to get up.

Sarah grabbed him by the arm. "No, that's okay."

"Don't you want coffee?"

She shook her head, tongue-tied again.

"What do you want, Sarah?" His voice was husky. His arms came around her. She tensed. This was it.

"Nothing to say? That's not like you." Jake began dropping soft kisses from her temple to her chin, pausing now and then to whisper outrageous things in her ear. All very enjoyable, but she was going to die if he didn't pop the question. Soon.

Before his mouth could cover hers in one of his mind-clouding kisses, she asked abruptly, "Wasn't there something you wanted to ask me?"

Jake drew back, a surprised look on his face.

"You said there was, before you left for San Antonio yesterday. Why did you go to San Antonio, anyway? It wasn't planned. I know because Leslie said you had a meeting with the programmers scheduled for yesterday, and you canceled it at the last minute. You never do things without a plan, so—"

Jake held up a hand, chuckling. "That's my Sarah. You've been so quiet all evening, I thought something was wrong. You could have caught the mystery virus that's been striking every other employee at Loganetics."

"I never get sick."

"Neither do I. We have that in common."

"Good." Sarah nodded. "Having things in common is good. But differences are good, too. Granny Brannan always said differences were what make things interesting. We are different in some ways. You're very organized. Neat. I'm not."

"No. I saw my kitchen."

Contrite, Sarah promised, "I'll clean it up."

"We'll clean it up together. Or we'll leave it for the maid." His arm came around her shoulders again. He gave her a suggestive squeeze. "If we think of something we'd rather do tonight."

Sarah shivered in delight. He must have been doing a little fantasizing, too. "You don't mind that I came here to cook dinner, do you? Your kitchen is so much bigger than mine. I used the key from under the flowerpot. I put it back."

"I don't mind your being in my home. That's why I told you about the key." He pulled her closer. "And, as a matter of fact, that's what I wanted to discuss with you."

"Me being in your home?" Sarah rested her head on his shoulder, grinning giddily.

"Exactly." Jake turned her around so she was facing him, keeping his hands on her shoulders. His grip was almost painful, but Sarah barely felt it. She slid her arms around his waist and looked deeply into his golden brown eyes. The intensity she saw there made her pulse race.

"I want you to live with me. For six months."

Sarah's mouth dropped open. She stared at him. "What?" He couldn't have said what she thought he had.

"I want us to live together."

"What?" she repeated stupidly.

Jake's brows snapped together. "I said—"

She jerked out of his arms. "I heard you. I didn't understand at first. I wasn't expecting a..." Proposition. Sarah's eyes widened as what Jake had said finally made sense. She'd just been propositioned by the man she loved.

Jake slid off the love seat and knelt in front of her. Taking both her hands in his, he said, "I've given this a lot of thought, Sarah. It will work. I know it will. Let me list the reasons...."

He was on his knees, but he didn't want to marry her. Hot tears began to sting the backs of Sarah's eyes. She blinked them away. She was not going to cry. Although it would serve him right if she did. According to Sarah's grandmother, a Brannan woman's tears could melt a heart of stone. Sarah was tempted to bawl her eyes out, but she had vowed not to use feminine tricks to trap Jake into a permanent relationship. A modern woman shouldn't need tricks—no matter what Granny Brannan said.

She swallowed the hysterical giggle bubbling in the back of her throat, and tried to stand. "I've got to go home now," she said.

Jake wouldn't let her get up. "Sarah, I'm sorry if I surprised you. But hear me out."

"Right now," she said, not as forcefully as she'd intended. She sank back down. She began taking deep breaths. Intent on calming her riotous emotions, she only half listened as her boss of eight months, her suitor—or so she'd thought—for the past three, systematically listed the reasons for them to cohabit for half a year.

"Living together has its good points and its bad points. As you said, we are different. Some of our differences may cause a few disagreements. But your grandmother was right. Other differences will make..."

How could she have been so naive? Jake Logan hadn't been courting her. He'd been seducing her. He wanted her to agree to an affair. An affair with a time limit, for heaven's sake. She drew her brows together and tried to concentrate.

Maybe she shouldn't have been caught off guard. Jake had told her, more often than she'd wanted to hear, that he didn't believe in long-term relationships. She hadn't taken him seriously. All men—all bachelors—said that, according to her sisters.

"I want you. And I know you want me."

He had her there. Jake made her pulse race and her toes curl every time he came near her.

"There is the risk of emotional attachment...."

No kidding? She'd taken that risk, and look what had happened. She was in love with the wrong man.

"That's where the time limit comes in. If we agree up front when to end the arrangement, we avoid any unpleasantness at the end of the—"

"That's enough!" She pulled her hands free and put them over her ears. "I will not listen to one more word."

Jake stopped his methodical listing of the pros and cons of the proposed affair. He hadn't omitted the cons, she had to give him that. Jake was always scrupulously fair. It was one of the first things she had admired about him. At the moment she couldn't remember the other reasons she'd fallen for him like a ton of bricks.

The man was nuts.

"What's the matter?" He put his hand on her forehead. "You're warm. I'm calling Dr. Johnson."

She shoved his hand away. "I am not sick! If I am hot it's because I'm mad. Insulted. Outraged." Her chin quivered. Hurt. But she wouldn't give him the satisfaction of knowing that, the jerk.

Rocking back on his heels, he eyed her warily. "Why?"

She rolled her eyes. "Figure it out for yourself, Mr. Computer-Head. I don't have a thing to say to you." She stood up. "Except goodbye."

"Sit down, Sarah. We haven't finished this discussion."

Sarah looked down at him. The man had just broken her heart and he wanted to talk about it? Fat chance. "Send me a message by E-mail. That is your preferred method of communication, isn't it?"

He got up off his knees and planted himself in front of her. "Sit!"

Sarah blinked, then sat. Jake never shouted. She tilted up her chin and glared at him. "I am not going to live with you. Not for six months. Not for six minutes. There. Now we have nothing else to talk about. Let me up!'' She tried standing again, but his hand on her shoulder kept her seated. He moved to sit next to her, but kept hold of her shoulders.

''Yes, we do.''

''No, we don't. I've said everything that needs to be said. I am leaving. Please, let me—''

Her voice broke. Mortified, Sarah stopped chattering and stared down at her hands.

''Look at me, Sarah.''

She shook her head and kept her eyes downcast. She didn't need to look at him. Sarah knew exactly how the frustrated anger she heard in his voice would be reflected in his golden eyes. His thick, dark brows would be drawn together in a frown. Without actually looking, she had no trouble seeing Jake's square jaw clench and his sensuous lips curl as he sat next to her.

If she looked at him, she might forget to be offended. Heaven help her, she was beginning to wonder if she should agree to his scandalous plan. Jake might look on an affair as the next logical step in a courtship. Sort of a beta test for marriage.

''Why won't you live with me?''

Maybe she should give him the benefit of the doubt. Cautiously, her heart in her throat, she raised her eyes. ''Live together as in the last step before getting married and living happily ever after?''

His eyes narrowed. ''I didn't say anything about marriage.''

The breath she'd been holding shuddered out of her in a mournful sigh. ''I didn't think so. Most marriages last longer than six months.''

"Not in my family," he muttered.

That distracted her momentarily. "What about your family?"

"Never mind. I have no intention of getting married. Ever." His voice was low and even, but forceful nonetheless. Jake meant what he said.

"Well, I guess that takes care of any little niggling doubt I might have had," she said. Her try for flippancy didn't work—she had whimpered the words. Swallowing the lump in her throat, she tried again. "Goodbye, Jake. It's been . . . interesting."

Sarah shrugged his hands off her shoulders and stood up. This time Jake didn't try to stop her.

"All right. I can see you're not ready to discuss the matter logically. We'll talk again tomorrow, after you've had time to calm down."

"I won't be here tomorrow. I'm going home. To Hamilton, to see my family. Tomorrow is the day before Thanksgiving, after all. Families do that, Jake. They get together on holidays."

"Do they? I wouldn't know," he said stiffly.

For a moment, he looked so sad and bewildered, she almost yielded to the temptation to throw herself in his arms and agree to do anything he asked. Before she made a fool of herself, the moment passed.

But Jake must have sensed her temporary weakness. He took her in his arms. "I'll go with you."

"You will not."

"You invited me. I'd forgotten what week this was, but you did ask me to your parents' home for Thanksgiving." He grinned smugly and pulled her close again.

"I invited you when I thought..." We would be announcing our engagement, she concluded silently.

"When you thought...?"

"It doesn't matter. I was wrong." Taking a firm grip on her emotions, Sarah faced him squarely. "Good-bye, Jake."

Jake stood in the doorway, watching Sarah's apple red Toyota until its taillights disappeared from view. What had gone wrong? He'd made a plan, executed it, and it had blown up in his face. Sarah had blown up in his face. He'd never seen her so angry. He'd never seen her angry, period.

Bewildered, Jake turned and went inside. He walked into the kitchen and groaned. Trust Sarah to leave things a mess for him to take care of. Clenching his fists, he told himself that was okay. He could deal with dirty dishes, and he needed something to keep him busy. He had to have time to get himself under control. Otherwise, he'd feel things he'd promised himself years ago he'd never feel again.

Lost. Lonely.

Jake clamped down on those thoughts. Memory lane was not a place he visited often, and tonight was not the night for a trip to the past. The present was what was giving him trouble, a present without Sarah.

She'd only been gone for two minutes. So how could the place seem so empty? How could he?

This emptiness wouldn't last. He'd fill it up with something. Work—what he'd always used to fill the empty spaces in his life. Loganetics was all he wanted, all he really needed. His business had been the most important thing in his life, before Sarah. It would be again, once he got her out of his system.

How could she have walked out? He'd thought the whole problem through very carefully before he'd asked her to move in with him. He turned on the hot water and began rinsing the dishes piled in the sink. As he worked, he reviewed his logic.

He wanted Sarah. She wanted him. It was past time to take their relationship to a more intimate level.

Jake arranged plates and silverware in their proper slots in the dishwasher. Although not absolutely necessary, living in the same place made sense. Alternating between his condo and her apartment wouldn't be convenient. He lived on Lake Austin. She lived miles away, close to the University of Texas. Going back and forth was bound to become a chore sooner or later.

Scouring the pots and pans, he continued testing his logic for flaws. If living together made sense, logic dictated that they should share his place. The condo was larger, with two bedrooms and a study. Her apartment had only one bedroom, a small one at that.

Jake put the pans in the dishwasher and turned it on. Leaning against the kitchen counter, he ticked off the reasons one more time. They all led to one logical conclusion. Sarah should move in with him.

So why had she turned him down?

Sarah always acted on her emotions. He preferred to rely on logic. Logically, a time limit would protect them both. Sarah would know in advance that their affair wasn't going to lead to marriage—realistic expectations had to be better than irrational romantic dreams. And he'd know exactly when she was leaving. It wouldn't be a surprise. He didn't deal well with surprises.

Sarah had been angry tonight. Angry and insulted. What had made her mad?

The evening had started well. Another delicious meal. His favorite pie for dessert. Mild necking on the patio, under the stars. When had things started to go wrong?

Immediately after he'd asked her to live with him, she'd looked shocked. Surprised. Maybe she didn't like surprises, either. On the other hand, she had listened to him... until he started explaining the six-month time limit. That was what had sent her running out the door.

Jake tried looking at it from her perspective. Sarah had made it crystal clear that she believed in love, or whatever the current politically correct term for lust was. He was halfway sure she thought she was in love with him. He hadn't argued with her about it. If she wanted to believe she was in love with him, he'd grin and bear it.

People illogical enough to believe in love probably wouldn't see the need for a time limit.

All right. He'd be willing to negotiate that point.

Having Sarah with him for as long as it lasted was important. Important enough that he could put up with some uncertainty about the length of the affair. As long as he reminded himself from time to time that Sarah wouldn't be around forever, he wouldn't be expecting the impossible. She was bound to leave, sooner or later, but maybe she would stay longer than six months. He'd based the time limit on the fact that his longest relationship to date had lasted only five months. But none of his previous lovers had been Sarah. Sarah was definitely one of a kind.

He still didn't know why he found her so damnably attractive. He had always preferred his women tall and curvaceous, with long legs and long hair. Sarah was barely three inches over five feet and the first time he'd seen her she'd been wearing her soft chestnut brown hair in a feminine version of a crew cut. She'd let it grow out to a short bob, and Jake liked to think it was because she was trying to please him. Women tried to please men they were attracted to. Sarah probably believed she'd always be attracted to him—in her terms, that she would always love him.

But he knew better. Pyramids lasted. Love didn't.

Sarah was an enthusiastic advocate of marriage, too, even though he'd told her from the beginning that he wasn't the marrying kind. She was always telling him stories about her sisters and their husbands, her mother and father. He should have anticipated that she'd bring up marriage. His stomach clenched. Marriage was out of the question. With his background—

Maybe he should have waited until they'd slept together before asking her to move in with him. He had wanted her almost from the first time he'd seen her, but he hadn't rushed her into bed. Something about Sarah had made him wary. Some long-buried instinct had tried to warn him she would disrupt his orderly existence. He'd ignored the warning and relied on logic as he'd always done. And look what had happened—logic and reason didn't stand a chance against Sarah.

Telling himself he was five times a fool if he let his actions be guided by anything as nonsensical as emotion, Jake walked into his bedroom. The closet door was standing open, revealing the space he'd cleared for Sarah's clothes. He'd emptied out a few drawers in the dresser for her, too.

He looked at the king-size bed. Sarah should have been there tonight. He tortured himself for a few minutes, imagining the things they would be doing to each other if she'd stayed. Then he took a cold shower and went to bed.

Alone.

"I love you, Sarah. Will you marry me?"

Jake jerked upright, heart pounding, drenched in a cold sweat. Fumbling for the light, he turned it on.

"Nightmare," he said. "You didn't propose."

The sound of his own voice reassured him, and after a few minutes his heartbeat slowed to normal. He turned off the light and closed his eyes, but sleep wouldn't come. He didn't often remember his dreams, and he hadn't had a nightmare since he was eighteen years old—the year his parents had told him he was on his own. Those nightmares had stopped once he'd made a plan for his future and acted on it.

A message from his subconscious—that's what this nightmare had been about. Sarah had thrown him a curve tonight. He hadn't expected her to turn him down. Just as he hadn't expected his mother and father to desert him financially when he was eighteen, even though they'd deserted him emotionally years before.

Dreams were not to be taken literally—everyone knew that. His subconscious did not want him to propose. It wanted him to make a plan to deal with Sarah, and act on it. He could do that.

But his plan would not include a wedding ring.

Chapter Two

Jake downshifted and let the Jaguar's powerful engine slow the car into a curve. He topped the hill and saw a low log building surrounded by a pecan orchard. The sign in front of the building said Brannan Country Store. Other signs and posters in the windows advertised pecans, both shelled and unshelled, candy, cakes and pies, as well as quilts and other handicrafts.

Sarah had told him her parents' house was down a long driveway behind the family store. Jake began looking for the turnoff. A few minutes later, he pulled up in front of a sprawling ranch house built of creamy Austin stone.

He sat in the car and looked around, taking in the neatly mowed lawn that gradually gave way to a meadow. Beyond the open field, the pecan trees marched in even rows down to the banks of a narrow river. No people were in view, but several other cars were parked on a wide pavement in front of the garage.

This was Sarah's home. Seeing her here, in the place where she'd grown up, with the people who'd raised her, was the first step in making his new plan. He'd thought he knew all about her. He'd classified Sarah as a woman of the nineties—independent, self-confident, secure in her own sexuality. But he'd missed something. He must have had insufficient data. He needed to know more about Sarah to avoid getting get blindsided by her emotional reactions to his logical and reasonable requests.

He wasn't very good at dealing with families—too little personal experience—but the Brannan family could be the key to understanding Sarah.

Jake got out of his car, walked to the front door and rang the bell. The door opened a few minutes later.

"Hello, Sarah." She was dressed in faded jeans and an orange-and-white University of Texas sweatshirt. She looked beautiful. She slammed the door in his face.

Or tried to. Reacting quickly, Jake managed to stop the door before it closed completely. He pushed it open and entered a wide hallway.

Sarah opened her mouth, but before she could speak he hauled her against him and gave her a resounding kiss. He couldn't let her talk, not yet. He could tell by the sparks in her eyes she hadn't planned to say anything he wanted to hear. He didn't stop kissing her until another woman appeared in the hallway.

Keeping his arms loosely around her waist, Jake looked over Sarah's head as the woman walked up behind her. "I'm Jake Logan. You must be one of Sarah's sisters. You were expecting me, I hope. Sarah invited me to spend Thanksgiving with her family."

The woman gave Sarah what looked like a chastising glance, but replaced it quickly with a warm smile for him.

"Of course we expected you! And you're right on time. I'm Nora Brannan, Jake."

He reached around Sarah and shook her hand. Sarah hadn't tried to move out of his arms. She seemed to be in shock.

"I have to confess that I'm Sarah's mother, not her sister. But flattery will get you a long way with a Brannan woman. Bring your young man along, Sarah. I've got to get the turkey on the table."

Nora Brannan hurried off. With a start, Sarah came out of her trance and bolted after her mother. Jake managed to grab her hand before she got away. Tangling his fingers with hers, he tugged her to a halt. "You're glad to see me. I can tell. Why don't you give me another kiss to prove it?"

"I'd sooner kiss a rattlesnake," she hissed, wiping her mouth with the back of her free hand. "Why are you here?" She jerked her other hand out of his and started down the hall again.

Jake caught up with her and took her by the arm. "You invited me. And it's time I met your family."

She slanted an incredulous look at him. "Why? Meeting families smacks of courtship and commitment, two things you've made clear you're not interested in."

"I'm interested in you, Sarah. That's reason enough to meet your family. What have you told them about me?"

"Not that you asked me to live with you. Dad won't be meeting you with his shotgun, if that's what you're worried about. They know you're my boss, and that we've gone out a few times, that's all." She tossed the words over her shoulder as she walked through an arched doorway.

Jake's brows came together in a fearsome scowl. That wasn't all, not by a long shot. As soon as they were alone, he'd take great pleasure in reminding her of that fact.

After a quick look around, however, Jake realized it might be a long time before he was alone with Sarah again.

The door opened into a large country kitchen complete with copper pots and an oak table big enough to seat a football team, with room left over for the cheerleaders. At the moment, six adults and four children were arranged around the table and there were still several vacant chairs.

Everyone was looking expectantly at him and Sarah. Sarah didn't seem to notice. She went to the table and sat down, leaving him standing in the doorway.

"Sorry if I got here at a bad time," Jake said. "Sarah—"

"Has forgotten her manners. Get another place setting, Sarah." Sarah's mother rose gracefully from her chair and came toward him. "Welcome, Jake. You don't mind if I call you Jake, do you? Let me introduce you to everyone."

Nora took him by the arm and led him to an empty seat next to the head of the table. "My husband, Wesley Brannan. Take this chair next to him. That way you'll be across the table from Sarah. Don't let Wesley put you off your feed. He looks mean, but he doesn't bite."

Jake shook hands with Sarah's father and sat down, forcing himself to concentrate on the introductions when what he wanted to do was focus all his attention on Sarah.

"This good-looking man is Vince Hall, Barbara's husband," said Nora, as she walked back to her chair at the opposite end of the table. "Barbara is next to him. She's Sarah's oldest sister."

Vince nodded a greeting and Nora continued the introductions. "The pint-size version across from Barbara is their son, Mack, and the pretty young thing next to him is his sister, Jennifer. The sourpuss sitting next to her is Sarah's other sister, Laura. The two rascals next to her are the twins, Ricky and Nicky, and last, but not least, Colt McCauley, Laura's husband."

Nora sat down. "Sarah, what's taking you so long? Jake must be starving."

Sarah slammed a plate on the table in front of him.

"Sarah! Be careful. That's Granny Brannan's best china!" said Nora.

Wesley Brannan, a huge man with grizzled gray hair and piercing blue eyes, looked Jake over as he carved the turkey. "So you're the man who saved our little girl from starvation."

"Daddy, I was not starving." Sarah handed silverware to Jake and sat down opposite him. She refused to meet his gaze. He didn't need to see her eyes to know she didn't think he was her rescuer.

"You were out of a job, young lady—and too stubborn to let your family help you out," said her father.

"I was self-employed, not unemployed."

"Oh? And how much were you paying yourself? Don't forget, I'm one of the bank directors. I know what your checking account balance was, young lady."

"That's an invasion of privacy!" Sarah objected, snitching a piece of turkey from under her father's nose.

"When did anyone in this family ever have any privacy?" asked Nora. "Sarah, stop playing with your food and pass Jake the cranberry sauce. Wesley, let the poor man eat in peace."

Wesley Brannan ignored his wife and continued his interrogation. "How did you get Sarah to work for you, Jake? I tried to tell her not to quit her job on the newspaper until she'd saved some money, but you know how she is."

Jake nodded, his mouth full of mashed potatoes and giblet gravy.

"Impulsive, that's my little sister Sarah," said Barbara.

"And illogical," added Jake. "She almost turned the job down, even though she needed the money. But I talked her into it."

"You shamed me into it." Sarah glared at him and handed him the bowl of corn bread dressing. "You told me my article about Loganetics' unreadable manuals hurt sales."

At least she was looking his way. He took the bowl from her, letting his fingers touch hers a fraction longer than was necessary. "Your magazine story did affect sales. But you didn't have to feel guilty about that—the article was accurate."

"Aha! You discovered Sarah's soft heart and used it against her. She really hates hurting people's feelings," said Wesley. "That's why she couldn't make a go of reporting hard news. So she went to work for you writing your software manuals to undo the damage she'd done."

"She's more than made up for the slight harm her magazine story caused. Her work is excellent," said Jake.

Wesley Brannan was right—Sarah was softhearted. He'd figured that out at their first meeting. By the end of the meal, Jake had learned a few things about Sarah he'd never known before. She got her chestnut brown hair, green eyes and quick mind from her mother, her propensity to tease from her father.

Touching was apparently a hereditary trait. Dinner had been punctuated by hugs and kisses, as well as by playful slaps and pinches, mostly originating with Sarah and her sisters.

No, he amended, only with Sarah and Barbara. The middle sister—what was her name? Laura. Laura hadn't said or done much during the meal. She'd hardly touched the delicious food. Laura had to be the quiet Brannan, Jake decided. A rarity in the family, obviously. The rest of them talked a mile a minute, just like Sarah. Though she certainly hadn't directed many words his way.

Nora Brannan was serving dessert—pumpkin and pecan pie—from the sideboard when the telephone rang. She answered it. "It's for you, Sarah. Rusty."

Sarah got up and took the telephone from her mother, then glanced at Jake. "I'll take it in the other room," she said, handing the receiver back to Nora.

Jake frowned. Who was Rusty?

Nora answered his unspoken question. "Rusty and Sarah went to school together—from kindergarten through college."

"He's an assistant football coach at UT now," added Wesley. "They're old friends."

"Friends?" muttered Jake, chewing that over as he waited for Sarah to come back.

After a few minutes, she returned to her seat across from him.

"What did Rusty want?" asked Wesley. "Where is he anyway? He was calling long-distance, wasn't he?"

"Yes, Daddy. He's right where he should be, in Austin getting ready for the game."

Jake narrowed his eyes. Rusty What's-his-name lived in Austin? If Rusty and Sarah were such good friends, shouldn't they have run into him at some point? He had met a few of her friends, mostly people Sarah had worked with at the *Austin Statesman*, but no one named Rusty.

Jennifer and Mack stood up, ending his speculation. "May we be excused?"

"Go ahead." Barbara leaned over and gave Jenny a quick kiss. "Take the twins with you."

The children left the room. Wesley Brannan leaned back in his chair, the picture of a contented patriarch.

He reached in his pocket and pulled out a cigar. "Jake? Have one?"

"No, thanks. I don't smoke."

Nora, walking by the head of the table with a bowl of leftover corn bread dressing, snatched the cigar from Wesley's hand. "Neither does he. At least not where I can see or smell the nasty things. Wesley, you know what the doctor said. You haven't been sneaking around, smoking behind my back, have you?"

"Now, Mother. I was only offering our guest a smoke out of politeness. And you know damn—'scuse me—darn well I haven't been sneaking around anywhere. How would I do that, with you in my pocket every minute?"

Nora set down the bowl with a clatter. Standing by the kitchen counter with her arms akimbo, she asked, "Are you complaining, Mr. Brannan?"

Wesley Brannan grinned a sheepish grin. "No, ma'am. I am not a complainin' man. Not a smoker, either." He turned back to Jake. "That woman said she'd never kiss me again if I ever lit up another stogie—a powerful incentive to quit." He leaned closer to Jake and said in a stage whisper, "You might as well know it, boy, if you're interested in Sarah—all Nora's daughters take after her. They're bossy, every one of them. Man's got to be smart to handle a Brannan woman."

Colt snorted. "I must be dumber than sin, then."

"I'd have to agree with that, Colt," said his wife. She wasn't teasing, Jake realized. Laura McCauley was seething with barely suppressed anger.

"Don't you talk to your husband that way, young lady," chided her father.

"Husband, hah! I don't have a husband. Just a man who shows up at my house now and then to change his shirt."

"Laura, this isn't the time or the place—"

"When is the time, Colt? I never see you anymore. You're never home."

"Hell's bells, honey. You make it sound like I'm out carousing. If I'm not at home, I'm at the office or in court and you know it."

"Don't honey me, you... you..." Laura stood up quickly and ran out on the patio.

"Trouble, Colt?"

Wesley Brannan's tone was mild, but Jake had the feeling the tone was deceptive. Sarah's father would take apart a man who hurt one of his daughters. He sneaked a guilty peek at Sarah. She was watching her brother-in-law.

She didn't look hurt, just annoyed. He could deal with that. There was no reason for him to feel guilty—he had no intention of hurting Sarah. Before he'd decided to ask Sarah to live with him, he'd spent hours figuring out a way to keep things casual and friendly from the beginning to the end. His six-month time limit had been specifically designed to make their final parting as painless as possible. Sarah couldn't blame him if she didn't see the logic of conducting an affair according to a prearranged schedule.

"Nothing I can't handle, Dad." Colt met Wesley's eyes directly. Whatever Wesley saw there must have reassured him. Jake could feel the tension between the two men dissipate.

"Are you spending too much time at the office?" asked Nora.

"Now, Mom, a man's got to provide for his family. It's not easy starting a law practice." Colt shoved his fingers through his hair. "Maybe I should have stayed with the district attorney's office a few more years, but what's done is done, and Laura's going to have to live with it." He stood up and joined his wife out on the patio.

As soon as the door closed behind him, the other family members all started talking at once.

"Well, what's that all about?"

"I knew something was wrong the minute I saw Laura's face."

"Colt's a hard worker—"

"It's not easy dealing with twins. Laura needs—"

"She shouldn't get so upset. Naturally, a man's got to—"

"Do what a man's got to do," chorused the Brannan women. They didn't sound as though they agreed with that philosophy. Fascinated, Jake leaned back in his chair, crossed his arms over his chest and watched the squabble escalate into a full-blown war between the sexes.

The battle ended in a draw soon after the coffee was served. While the rest of the family adjourned to the den to watch the last quarter of the Thanksgiving Day football game between Dallas and Washington, Sarah helped Barbara clear the table.

They were alone in the kitchen when Barbara asked, "What is going on with you and Jake?"

Stacking plates in the sink, Sarah ignored Barbara. She wasn't ready to play the Brannan sisters' version of twenty questions. She hadn't been able to think straight since Jake had showed up on the Brannan doorstep.

Barbara waved a soapy hand under her nose. "Hello? Talk to me, Sarah."

"I don't know what you mean."

"I mean why are you being so mean to the man? How can you ignore those smoldering looks he's been directing your way? Jake obviously wanted to be alone with you, and you turned him down to wash dishes."

"Don't you want my help?"

"Sure, but it's not like you to volunteer. Usually we have to use force to get you to clean anything."

"Do not."

"Do, too. Don't try to change the subject, Sarah. I repeat. What is going on with you and Jake?"

"Nothing's going on. He's a rat."

"Oh, please. Last month when we had lunch, he was Mr. Wonderful. You couldn't say enough about him. Jake Logan, computer wizard, successful entrepreneur, benevolent employer. What were all those benefits you listed? On-site day care. Paid maternity and paternity leave."

Sarah sniffed. "I don't have any use for maternity leave or day care. Or Jake Logan."

"Uh-huh. Then why did I get the distinct impression you were planning to use some of those fringes in the not-so-distant future?" Barbara lifted Sarah's left hand out of the soapy dishwater. "No engagement ring. The way you were talking, I halfway expected to see one. What happened?"

Jerking her hand back, Sarah glared at her sister. "He didn't propose. There. Are you satisfied?"

"Maybe he's waiting until next month. An engagement ring makes a nice Christmas present."

"He's not going to propose next month or next year. He doesn't plan on getting married. Ever. To anyone. He told me so very emphatically Tuesday night."

"And then he shows up here on Thursday. Looks like a lovers' quarrel to me."

"We're not lovers."

"Not yet."

"Not ever. I told you—that's not going to happen."

"What was the fight about?"

"We didn't fight. Jake is much too civilized to f-fight." Sarah couldn't hold back the tears any longer. "He just b-broke my heart, that's all."

Barbara hugged her, then grabbed a dish towel and handed it to her. "Oh, Sarah, I'm so sorry. What did he do, baby?"

Sarah took the towel and dried her eyes. Crying over Jake Logan was the last thing she wanted to do. He didn't deserve her tears. Taking a few moments to compose herself, she told Barbara the sad story.

"He said he had something important to talk to me about. Naturally, I thought he was going to propose. So I fixed the most wonderful dinner—candlelight, chocolate meringue pie, the works. And then he asked me to... to move in with him. He didn't even tell me he loves me. He just w-wants me."

"And you love him, don't you?" asked Barbara.

Sarah nodded, drying her eyes again. She had to stop bawling before the rest of the family heard her and joined in the conversation.

"And he has the nerve to show up here? He thinks he can seduce you right under your family's collective noses? You were right, Sarah. He is a rat." Barbara began untying her apron. "Wait until I tell Vince and Colt—"

"No! I don't want them to know."

"Know what?" asked Laura, strolling into the kitchen. She sat down at the table. "Football game's over. The Cowboys won."

"Where are the boys?" asked Barbara.

"The little boys are taking naps, finally." Laura nibbled absently on a wilted celery stick. "They've sure been cranky lately. You don't suppose they could be coming down with something, do you?"

Barbara snorted. "Not likely, not the way they put the food away. Where are the big boys?"

"Vince took Colt and Jake to see your new bull. They were going to drop Jennifer and Mack off at the Hall place on the way so they can have their second Thanksgiving dinner there. What have you two been talking about?"

"This and that and bacon fat," said Barbara.

"Sarah's awfully quiet. And she's washing dishes. What's wrong with her?"

Barbara nudged Sarah in the ribs with her elbow. When Sarah looked at her, she raised a quizzical eyebrow.

"You can tell her," mumbled Sarah. "I just don't want the whole family in here grilling me."

Patting Sarah on the shoulder, Barbara said to Laura, "Sarah's having problems with Jake. She wants to get married. He doesn't."

"Oh, is that all? Another man who thinks he's not ready to commit. Well, we've been there, haven't we?" Laura winked at Barbara. "What are we going to do about it?"

Sarah threw up her hands. "*We* aren't going to do anything. *I'm* not going to do anything. I tried. I failed. Time to move on."

"No, sugar," drawled Laura. "Not yet. Not when you two steam up my contacts every time I get near you. Your Jake is some man."

"He's not my Jake. He never was."

"But you want him to be," said Barbara. "You're in love with him."

"I'll get over it. Won't I?"

"You won't have to," said Barbara. She poured herself a cup of coffee and joined Laura at the table. "Not after Laura and I show you a few tricks. Jake will be begging you to marry him."

Sarah's heart began to beat a little faster. "I don't want him to marry me. Not if he doesn't love me."

"That goes without saying. But, if you ask me, that part's already taken care of. He may not want to admit it, though. Some men have trouble saying the words," Laura observed.

"I tried telling myself that was the problem, but I was wrong. It's not just the words he has trouble with—it's the whole idea. Jake told me he doesn't believe in love. I didn't listen to him, but I should have. Jake always means what he says, and he says emotions are illogical."

"Ah." Barbara said as she and Laura exchanged glances. "The Mr. Spock syndrome. That's a tough nut to crack, all right."

"Anyone want this last piece of pecan pie?" When both her sisters shook their heads, Sarah put the pie on a plate and brought it to the table. Sitting down, she told Barbara, "But it's over, so I don't have to crack that particular nut."

"Oh, no. It's not over," said Barbara.

"Of course it isn't. You've only begun to fight." Laura took the pie away from her. "Eating too much isn't going to make you feel better. It's only going to make you fat." She took a bite of pie.

Barbara put her elbows on the table, resting her chin on her hands. "Turning down his proposition was the right thing to do. But that was only the first step. You can bet your bottom dollar he's not through trying to convince you to move in with him."

"The fact that he followed you into the bosom of your family is a very good sign," added Laura, waving the fork.

Barbara took the fork away from Laura and helped herself to a bite of pecan pie. "If Dad knew Jake's intentions were less than honorable, there's no telling what he would do. Whatever it was, you can bet Jake wouldn't enjoy it."

Sarah squirmed. "I don't want anyone to beat him up."

"No one's going to use a shotgun to get him to the altar," said Laura. "Not yet, anyway. Now, let's get back to the point I was trying to make. If he followed you here, he must care about you."

Sarah shook her head. "He just wants me, that's all. Jake is very single-minded when he wants something. And he has the reputation for always getting what he wants. He probably looks on me as some kind of a challenge."

"That's okay. We can work with that. Accept the challenge and give him what he wants—after you get the ring on your finger," Barbara advised.

"Easy for you to say."

"No one said it would be easy. But Brannan women always get their man."

"No, we don't." Sarah sighed. "I didn't get mine."

"You will. With a little help from us." Laura gave her a saucy grin. "Once we show you how to play the game of love, he won't stand a chance."

Sarah bristled. "I'm not tricking him into marriage. I don't play games."

"Jake does. He wanted you to play house," Barbara pointed out.

"By his rules," added Laura. "Your instincts were right on the money to turn him down. It won't be easy getting him to say the M word, not if he thinks he can get all the benefits of marriage without the license and the preacher. Remember Granny Brannan's words of wisdom? Men are slow, simple creatures. Give them what they want too soon and they think that's all they want."

"Are we talking about love or sex?" asked Sarah.

"Both," said Barbara. "Men confuse the two, you know. Sleep with a man and he's sure he's in love. Until morning. Then he realizes it was only lust. A woman has to teach her man that love means trust and commitment before she surrenders."

"I don't remember Granny saying all that. What she said was, 'If a man can get milk for the asking, he's not going to buy the cow.'"

"So we embellished it a little. We speak from personal experience, don't forget. Trust me, little sister. Our kind of tricks never hurt any man—not for long, anyway. Ask Vince and Colt if you don't believe us."

"I know, Barbara, but—"

"No buts. All's fair in love and war. And this is both." Barbara reached over and took the last bite of pie. "Men think marriage means they have to take care of us, and they just naturally shy away from all that responsibility. You just have to show Jake it's a two-way street—that you'll take care of him, too."

"Colt is carrying his sense of responsibility to extremes," Laura said, sighing. "I never see him, much less take care of him."

"Of course you do," said Sarah. "Who's cooking his meals?

"Half the time he eats a sandwich at the office."

"I suppose he washes his own socks and underwear," Barbara commented dryly.

"No, I do that. And I take his suits to the cleaners and his car to the car wash. Not to mention raising his children. They barely recognize him."

"We'll take care of your problem later, Laura. Right now, let's get back to Jake and Sarah. Inviting him here for Thanksgiving was a good move—nothing like a little positive show and tell," said Barbara. "Seeing three happy marriages—"

"Two," said Laura ruefully with a sigh. "Mine's no picnic right now. Me fighting with Colt probably put Jake off marriage for good."

"I don't think so. Jake seemed to enjoy the whole thing," said Barbara. "He even jumped into the fight, there at the end."

"Yeah. On Colt's side," Laura pointed out.

Sarah drew her brows together, remembering Jake's defense of Colt. Of course, Jake did have workaholic tendencies himself, but he'd curbed them when they started spending time together. She turned her attention back to Barbara. "He's been awfully quiet today."

Barbara snorted. "What did you expect? Poor man couldn't get a word in edgewise. Not with all the Brannans talking at once. And you ignored him."

"My kids weren't exactly an advertisement for family life, either," Laura added mournfully. "Ricky and Nicky have been acting like brats all day."

"The twins are probably picking up bad vibes from you and Colt. You two better come to an understanding soon," cautioned Barbara.

"I know. It's just so hard, sometimes, living with an ambitious attorney. I miss my rodeo cowboy."

"When he was a rodeo cowboy, you couldn't wait for him to settle down and become a hardworking family man," Sarah reminded Laura. She got up and took the now empty pie plate to the dishwasher.

"What's that old saying about being careful what you wish for?" Laura sighed.

"You know what Granny Brannan would say. You made your bed, now lie in it."

"I'd be happy to, if Colt was there with me. I never intended to lie in my bed alone."

"You're not thinking of divorce, are you?" Sarah bit her lip. There had never been a divorce in the Brannan family before. But this was the nineties, the decade of disposable families.

Laura's eyes widened. "Are you kidding? I'm not letting that man of mine go. Not after I worked so hard to rope and tie him. We'll work things out."

"I know you will. So, let's concentrate on helping Sarah lasso Jake."

"Has he seen you in a sexy swimsuit?" asked Laura.

"It's November."

"Oh, right." Laura frowned. "A sexy dress?"

"No. I don't have a sexy dress. I don't have a dress, period. You know that."

"Get one. Get several. And Rusty—you can use him to make Jake jealous. He didn't like it when you took that call from him today. What did Rusty want, anyway?"

"A ride to Austin Sunday. He's driving his folks back here tonight after the game. He said his dad doesn't like to drive at night anymore."

"Did you tell Jake?"

"No. It's none of his business."

"Oh, honey, you've got lots to learn. Now, here's what you do...."

Chapter Three

A few miles away, at the Lazy H Ranch, Jake leaned against a corral fence watching Vince Hall and Colt McCauley trade macho glares with a big red bull. Jake thought the bull was winning.

"He's got the look," said Vince.

"Should we tell him?" Colt asked.

"Hell, yes. I can't stand to see a man suffer."

Jake turned to look at the other men. They were both staring at him. He'd thought they were talking about the bull.

"She won't," Vince said cryptically.

"Won't what?" asked Jake, bewildered.

"Go to bed with you."

"A Brannan woman won't indulge in hanky-panky," explained Colt. "Not until you put a ring on her finger—third finger, left hand."

"She won't?"

"Not ever. Not even if she loves you," said Vince. "Especially not if she loves you."

Vince nodded. "Barbara put me through hell before I finally wised up and popped the question."

"Ditto," said Colt, frowning at the bull. "No ring, no satisfaction."

"If you're not interested in marriage, you might as well write Sarah off."

"I'll keep that in mind." Jake tried unsuccessfully to suppress a grin. Anyone could see Sarah was nothing like her sisters.

Vince and Colt exchanged glances. "He doesn't believe us."

"How long have you known Sarah?" asked Vince.

"Eight or nine months."

"And how long have you two been going together?"

"Three months."

Vince slapped Jake on the back. "Son, you've only begun to suffer."

"You may be right," Jake said thoughtfully. But any pain he was feeling would end as soon as Sarah moved in with him. Ringless.

Vince gave Colt a quizzical look, then turned back to the bull. Jake let their voices fade into the background as he analyzed what they'd told him.

Was that why Sarah hadn't agreed to an affair with him? Because she was waiting for a proposal? Jake shook his head. That couldn't be right. He'd made it scrupulously clear from the beginning that he wasn't the marrying kind. Sarah had listened to what he'd said about marriage, and she hadn't refused to go out with him.

She was twenty-six. If she were like her sisters, she would be married by now. She wanted a career as a free-lance writer. And she wanted him. He'd bet his stock options on that. Even if Sarah planned on getting married someday, whenever she met Mr. Right, she had do something in the meantime. It might as well be with him. Jake scowled at the bull. He didn't like thinking about Sarah's Mr. Right.

The bull snorted and pawed the ground.

Vince chuckled. "Now you've definitely got the look—frustrated and mad as hell. You might as well give up and buy the ring."

"I don't think so. I've told Sarah I'm not interested in marriage."

Colt and Vince exchanged knowing looks. "That's like showing a red flag to our friend here," said Vince, pointing to the bull. "A Brannan woman thrives on a challenge. Has she snuggled up to you on the dance floor yet?"

"Wearing a dress no decent woman should wear in public?" added Colt, groaning.

"I never took her dancing. And I don't think Sarah owns a dress." Sarah favored slacks and sweaters, at work and after hours.

"No sexy dresses?"

"No sensuous dances?" Colt shook his head. "I don't understand. Sarah sure acts like she's interested in you. She did invite you home to meet her family."

The three men watched the bull in silence for a few minutes.

"Come to think of it, Sarah's never done things exactly like her sisters. She follows her own drummer," Vince said thoughtfully.

"That's true. Barbara was a cheerleader, and homecoming queen. Laura, too. Sarah was captain of the debate team and editor of the high school newspaper. She was as popular as her sisters, but in her own way."

"Colt is right about that. Another difference—Sarah has always wanted to be a writer. And she did turn down Rusty. Maybe she's not interested in marriage."

"Maybe not," said Jake. He waited a full three seconds before asking nonchalantly, "I thought she and Rusty were friends. What did she turn down, exactly?"

"A proposal. They are friends, but they dated for a little while, right after they went down to Austin to go to college. You know how it is—two small town kids away from home for the first time. Guess they kinda clung to each other until they got over being homesick."

"I went away to boarding school when I was eight. I didn't cling to anyone," Jake said, his voice cold and remote. Clinging didn't keep people around, not if they were ready to move on.

"Oh," said Vince, scuffing his boot in the dust.

Vince and Colt looked uncomfortable. People always looked uncomfortable when Jake talked about his childhood. Usually he knew better than to bring it up, but thinking about Sarah and Rusty clinging to each other had short-circuited his brain.

Colt cleared his throat. "Well, nothing serious ever developed. Between Rusty and Sarah, I mean. They weren't ready to settle down back then."

"I guess it's possible she's still not ready to settle down," added Vince. "She's working for you, isn't she? Maybe her career is more important to her than a family."

Vince pulled a stem out of a bale of hay and chewed on it for a minute. "Her sisters, now, are a different story. They never were interested in careers. Neither one of them ever held down a job—other than helping out at the family store. They've all done that from time to time. Barbara works at the store most days, now that Jenny and Mack are both in school. But you couldn't call that a career."

"Laura never wanted anything except to be a wife and mother," Colt said, a forlorn look on his face. "So why won't she relax and let me be the breadwinner?"

"Who knows? Women—can't live with 'em, can't live without 'em, hey, pardner?" Vince slapped his Stetson against his leg, and turned back to the bull. "So what do you think, Colt? Are you going to get your law office organized soon?"

Jake rested his arms on the top rail of the corral and let Colt and Vince rehash the day's argument. He didn't have anything more to contribute to that conversation. Colt didn't seem to be worried about Laura leaving him, though. That was something he'd analyze later. Now he wanted to concentrate on what he'd learned about Sarah.

He had been right. Sarah wasn't old-fashioned like her sisters. She was a modern woman. She might have mentioned marriage the other night, but that was probably some kind of female reflex. Like the one that made women dress up lust with hearts and flowers and call it love.

He hadn't worked at seducing Sarah because she hadn't seemed to want the usual candy and flowers routine. Apparently Barbara and Laura had made Vince and Colt jump through all kind of feminine hoops—including the one shaped like a wedding ring—before they finally got what they wanted. Sarah must have witnessed her sisters' courtships. She probably missed the steps he'd tried to skip.

Jake stirred restlessly. The last thing he wanted to do was waste time on romantic nonsense. But if that was what it would take to get Sarah to live with him, he'd try doing things her way. For a while. He'd take Sarah dancing, to the theater, send her flowers—she'd have to see he cared about her, as much as he'd ever cared about any woman.

But it wouldn't be all Sarah's way. He would make love to her, and soon. He had to. Vince and Colt had one thing right—he was suffering. His body was learning a whole new way to ache. But the pain was only temporary. After their affair was under way, Sarah would see the logic of living together. After all, it was the sensible thing to do. They already spent most of the hours away from work together. Once they were lovers, she'd have no reason to live anywhere but with him. All he had to do was get close enough to convince her to give him another chance.

He'd start tonight.

With a jolt, Jake realized that Colt and Vince had stopped talking and were looking at him expectantly.

"Did I miss something?"

"We just asked who you'll be rooting for tonight—Texas or A&M?"

"I don't know."

"Vince went to A&M. Sarah and I went to Texas. What's your alma mater?"

"MIT. And Wharton School of Business. Guess I'll be neutral."

"No way," said Vince. "Neutrality is not an option."

Jake shrugged. "No problem. I'll let Sarah tell me who to cheer for."

"Hot-diggity-dog! Another Longhorn fan," crowed Colt. "The Aggies will be outnumbered for sure this year, old son." Colt slapped Vince on the shoulder.

"Maybe in the living room, but not in Austin. On the football field, the Twelfth Man will win the day." He looked at his watch. "We'd better be getting back if we want to see the kickoff."

Football; feminine tricks—he'd had enough of that kind of talk. As they walked back to Vince's Bronco, Jake changed the subject to something that wasn't a foreign language to him. "Colt, did I hear you say something about getting your law office organized? What kind of computers do you have?"

"An IBM clone."

"Only one?"

"Yeah. Wouldn't have that one except my secretary insisted. Nobody uses typewriters anymore, it seems. And we do use Loganetics WordMaster. Sarah made sure of that."

"We're developing a new program that might save you some time. When I get back to the office, I'll send you the literature. If it looks interesting to you, maybe we can work something out. We'll be needing some real-life test sites soon."

"Time is what I need more of. Sell any of that?"

"Time-savers. That's what we're working on. Loganetics TimeMaster." Jake continued telling Colt and Vince about Loganetics's newest product on the way back to the Brannan home.

When they arrived, the kitchen table was covered with platters and bowls, and everyone was busily making turkey sandwiches or filling paper plates with leftovers.

"Dallas," said Barbara.

"San Antonio," said Laura.

"Waco," said Sarah.

"What are you girls arguing about now?" asked Vince.

"We're not arguing and we're not girls." Barbara kissed him on the cheek. "We are women, hear us roar, and we're discussing where to go shopping tomorrow."

"I can't go to Dallas or Waco," wailed Laura. "We've got to get back to San Antonio tomorrow morning. The legal eagle here has an afternoon appointment with a new client."

"Shopping is better in Dallas. I want to go to Neiman's," insisted Barbara.

"Waco's closer. And we can take the kids to the Texas Ranger Museum."

"No kids. This is a serious shopping expedition. The kids can stay here and help out at the store. Laura, I'll drive you back to San Antonio Saturday or Sunday."

Laura looked at Colt. "Is that okay, honey?"

"Sure. I never meant for you and the twins to cut the holiday short."

"Isn't the Friday after Thanksgiving the busiest shopping day of the year?" asked Jake, taking a turkey leg off the platter. "Why would you want to shop tomorrow?"

Three pair of eyes pinned him with incredulous stares.

"Because," they said in unison.

"They've always done it," explained Nora. "At first, Wesley and I would take them to a mall in Dallas or San Antonio to see Santa Claus. Then, when Barbara and Laura were in high school, the three of them began going on their own. Not to Dallas or San Antone, you understand—too far for them to go by themselves. They'd go to Waco and do their Christmas shopping, and buy their dresses for the holiday dances and parties."

"I never bought dresses," said Sarah.

"You will tomorrow. In Dallas," Barbara said.

Jake nibbled on his turkey leg and wondered why Sarah needed a dress. Then he remembered—the office Christmas party. The invitations had gone out by E-mail on Monday. Sarah was buying a dress to wear to the party.

He almost choked as a vision of Sarah in a silky, sexy dress popped into his mind. What if Vince and Colt's predictions were about to come true? Sweat broke out on his forehead as he imagined Sarah in his arms, dancing a mind-destroying, sensuous dance with him.

No. The other men had to be wrong. They'd agreed Sarah wasn't anything like her sisters. She wouldn't resort to feminine tricks. Not his Sarah.

Sarah stared blindly in the bathroom mirror as she vigorously brushed her teeth. She'd go to Dallas tomorrow, because it was a family tradition, and because Barbara and Laura had insisted she needed a new wardrobe. So she'd go and buy sexy dresses. And seductive perfume. And silky panty hose. But she wouldn't wear them. No matter what Barbara and Laura said, dresses and perfume weren't going to make her irresistible. If Jake hadn't fallen in love with the real her, he wouldn't fall for a new, improved, sexually explicit version.

Would he?

She stuck her toothpaste-covered tongue out at her reflection. Even if Jake were the kind of man to be taken in by superficialities, which he wasn't, she was not desperate enough to resort to sordid tricks to get him to propose.

Was she?

Darn. Barbara and Laura had succeeded in further confusing her—and she'd already done a pretty good job of that all by herself. They were convinced she shouldn't give up on Jake. But their hearts wouldn't be the ones ground into heartburger if she failed a second time.

Barbara and Laura weren't the only family members trying to sabotage her resolve to leave Jake alone. Her own mother had insisted that he spend the night. When he'd protested—weakly, she thought—that he hadn't come prepared to stay, her father had loaned him a pair of pajamas and scrounged up a new toothbrush. Even Ricky and Nicky got into the act, agreeing to spend the night with their cousins so he could have their bed in Barbara's old room. The room that shared the bath with Sarah's room.

Sarah eyed the door warily. There wasn't a lock. Her father had removed it when she was nine, after she locked herself in the bathroom to keep from being taken to the dentist. She shook her head. Jake had been trying to get her alone all evening, but he wouldn't follow her into the bathroom. She didn't want to be alone with him until she'd decided what she was going to—

The bathroom door opened.

"Jake! Get out of here!" she sputtered, dribbling water and toothpaste onto her chin.

"No. I want to talk to you, and this is the only place we can have a private conversation." He took a hand towel from the rack and patted her chin dry, then closed the lid on the toilet. "Have a seat."

"I will not." She tried to move past him to the door to her room. Before her hand touched the doorknob she found herself sitting—on Jake's lap. "Let me go!" she said, squirming furiously.

"Settle down. This won't take long, if you'll cooperate."

She stilled. "What won't take long? If you think I'm going to participate in a quickie in the bathroom—"

"We'll have to try that sometime," he said, nuzzling her neck. "But not now. I just want to talk to you." He nibbled on her earlobe. "Mmm. Better than leftover turkey," he murmured, his warm breath tickling her neck.

Sarah felt herself melting. Holding herself stiffly, she stared at the ducks on the shower curtain. "Say what you want to say. And talk fast."

"I want—"

"I know you think you want me, but you'll get over it. I got over wanting you."

"So soon?" He put his hand on her nape and held her head in place while he kissed her breathless.

"Stop," Sarah said weakly, forcing herself to glare at him. She had to get mad, and fast. Anger was the only emotion it was safe to feel around Jake. If she wasn't careful, she'd be taking him by the hand and leading him into her bedroom.

"Now can I tell you what I want?"

She nodded.

"I want you to take as much time as you need on your shopping trip. Don't feel like you have to come back to work on Monday." He continued to drop tiny kisses on her face, from her temple to her chin and back again.

"What makes you think I'm coming back to work at all?" she gasped, trying to find a way to stop him before she gave in and began kissing him back.

That got his attention. He stopped kissing her and asked, "Why wouldn't you come back to work?"

Struggling into a more or less upright position, she looked him in the eyes. "It might be awkward, don't you think? Working together now that we've broken up?" Shaking her head mournfully, Sarah sighed. "I should have listened to all that advice against romancing the boss. But I didn't. So I'm seriously considering quitting."

Jake stood up abruptly, taking her with him. As they stood face-to-face, she watched his eyes and tried to gauge his reaction to her half-serious remarks. He looked angry. And worried.

Amazing.

Barbara and Laura had been right. Subterfuge worked. Chalk one up for the Brannan woman's approach.

"You can't quit. You haven't finished the manual on TimeMaster."

"No, I haven't, but—"

"You're the only one who can finish it on schedule. A new writer would have to start from scratch. If we blow the deadline, a lot of people will lose their bonuses."

"Are you trying to make me feel guilty?"

"Damn straight. You signed an employment contract, remember? I'll do whatever it takes to get you to honor your commitment. Including sue you for breach of contract if you try to leave."

"Oh, yeah?" she blustered. Not the most brilliant response, but Jake's kisses had curdled her brain cells.

"Oh, yeah, Sarah. Whatever it takes." He took her in his arms again and held her immobile.

"Don't threaten me!"

"No threat. I'm telling you the way it's going to be. You're coming back to work. And you don't have to worry about it being awkward, because it won't be. We haven't broken up. Nothing's broken that can't be fixed. I'll see you first thing Monday morning."

"I thought you said I could have more time off if I needed it."

"You won't need it. Now that I think about it, your sisters will have to get back to their children, won't they? And Vince said Barbara works at the family store. You were planning to come back on Sunday all along, weren't you?"

She glared at him. "Why did you offer me more time, if you didn't mean it?"

"I was prepared to be without you for a few more days before you said you were going to quit. But now I'd be a wreck wondering when—if—you were going to show up. You don't want me to suffer like that, do you?"

"A wreck? Goodness. How about that?" She couldn't help smiling.

"I don't believe it! You do want me to suffer." He gave her a small shake. "Are you coming back to work, or not?"

"I honor my commitments, Mr. Logan. I'll see you Monday morning."

"Good. We'll go to lunch and talk about us."

"No lunch. There is no us."

"There was and there will be again, and we'll be better together than we were before. Trust me."

Trust him to break her heart twice, if she gave him the chance. Well, she wouldn't. She was a Brannan woman, and no man, not even Jake Logan, was going to break her heart. Not without a fight.

Sarah stopped trying to wiggle out of Jake's arms. Letting her soft body mold itself to his hard frame, she wrapped her arms around his neck and looked up at him through her lashes.

"Trust *me,* Jake. It really is over between us. Kiss me goodbye."

Chapter Four

"Sorry about the game. Darn those Aggies, anyway." Sarah slanted a glance at her passenger. He had the seat in its full-recline position and appeared to be sleeping. She couldn't be sure of that, since his cowboy hat was covering his face.

"Rusty? Are you awake?"

Rusty grunted. That was a start, but a long way from the conversation she wanted. Her head was chock-full of advice from her sisters, but she needed a man's point of view. Unfortunately, this man hadn't said two words since they'd left the Hansen house fifty miles back. Why was she cursed with these strong, silent types? First Jake, now Rusty. She reached over and squeezed his knee.

"Are you going to sleep all the way back to Austin?"

"Pro'ly."

One more word. Great. A word every twenty or thirty miles might get her a whole sentence by the time they got to Austin. What would make him sit up and take notice?

Sarah let her gaze drift over the rolling hills dotted with cedar trees and cottonwood groves. Not the scenery. They'd seen it too many times, going to and from Austin, to plays and football games when they were children, to college after they'd grown up.

Rusty had been her honorary big brother since her birthday party the year she'd turned five. The one time they'd experimented with being more than friends had been a mistake, one they'd both recognized almost immediately. She'd never figured out exactly why they'd never be more than friends, though. Objectively, Rusty was everything she could want—honorable, trustworthy and kind, with just enough of the devil in him to keep him from being Boy Scout boring. There was nothing wrong with the package all those virtues were wrapped up in, either.

The problem was, he wasn't Jake.

But he could help her with Jake, if she could get him to talk. Maybe food would wake him up. She eyed the six-foot-four hulk sprawled next to her. Rusty did like to eat. "Want to stop in Marble Falls for lunch? At the Bluebonnet Café?"

"'kay with me." He shifted in his seat and snored.

So much for subtlety. Sarah punched him in the ribs. "Wake up!"

"What was that for?" Rusty tilted his hat back and glared at her.

"I need to talk to you."

He moved the seat to an upright position and rubbed his eyes. "What do you want to talk about?"

"Men."

"Aw, hell, Sarah," Rusty groaned. "What's he done to you?"

"Who?" she asked innocently. "I said men, not a man."

"I know, but you mean one particular man. Women never want to talk about men in general with another man. You told me that when we were in high school."

Sarah narrowed her eyes. "You know too much, and it's mostly my fault. I told you things no man should know."

"It didn't help. I still don't understand women."

"Women? Or one particular woman?"

Rusty groaned again. "Leslie Simmons. The woman you introduced me to. You set me up, Brannan."

"And you should thank me for it. Leslie is beautiful, intelligent, funny. What more could you want?"

"Not a damn thing."

"Well, then, what is the problem?" Sarah slanted another glance at Rusty. He was staring out the window, a glum look on his face. She felt a pang of guilt. She hoped her good-intentioned attempt at matchmaking hadn't been a mistake. "What has Leslie done?"

"I asked her to marry me and she turned me down."

Sarah bristled. "What's wrong with her? You two are perfect for each other."

"I know that. I thought she did, too, once she agreed we should live together."

Sarah turned her head and stared at Rusty. "You and Leslie are living together?"

Rusty grabbed the wheel. "Watch the road, Sarah. You almost missed that curve."

"Sorry, but you shouldn't drop surprises like that into the conversation with no warning. I didn't know you and Leslie were living together. She didn't tell me and neither did you. What kind of friends are you, anyway, keeping something like that a secret?"

"It is kind of personal, Sarah. Besides, I thought the whole world would know before Thanksgiving. I planned for us to announce our engagement Thursday night."

Sarah almost lost control of the car again. After taking a few calming breaths, she resolutely kept her eyes on the road. "That's funny—"

"No, it's not."

"Not funny-ha-ha—funny-peculiar. I wanted to announce my engagement this week, too."

"So it is one particular man you want to talk about."

"All right, all right. I admit it. But first, I want to know why you moved in with Leslie."

"I had this dumb idea that if she got to know me up close and personal, she'd get over being so. . .scared. Geez, I hate to say it out loud. The woman loves me, and she's afraid of me."

"Don't be silly. She may be afraid of getting hurt again, of making another mistake. You know what kind of man she was married to before—"

"Yeah, I know. A low-down dirty dog. But I'm not like that."

"Of course you're not. Everyone knows you're a marshmallow."

Rusty curled his lip. "Soft and gooey? Great. I'll never make defensive coordinator if Coach thinks I'm a marshmallow."

"Don't change the subject. This is not the time to talk about football. Relationships. That's the topic of the hour. Why doesn't Leslie want to get married?"

"Don't ask me. I love her, she loves me. I think. But she won't even talk about it. Says I'm putting too much pressure on her. I swear if I had any place to go, I'd leave. But moving's such a pain in the butt, and there's no place available now. No place close to the university, anyway. I'll have to wait until next semester to make my move."

"What kind of move? Have you given up on her?"

"Not by a long shot. I want to tell her, 'marry me or I'm leaving.' That would do the trick. Maybe not right away, but she'd miss me after I was gone. But I can't give her an ultimatum until I've got someplace to go to."

Sarah risked a quick glance at Rusty. They were both ready to use trickery and deceit to get what they wanted, but he sounded a lot more confident than she felt. Especially since Barbara and Laura weren't around to give her pointers and egg her on. "That sounds risky," she said.

"Nothing risky about it. You have to have a game plan, and you have to know your opponent." He punched the air with his index finger, to emphasize his point. "That way you can anticipate her next move and come up with a counterattack. The way it is now, Leslie's got what she wants—me, without strings. I should never have moved in with her. As long as I make things easy for her, she's never going to marry me."

"So you're going to start playing games?"

"I'm always playing games. That's how I make my living. Besides, she started it. Leslie plays hard to get better than any woman I ever knew. The woman drove me crazy before she'd agree to go out with me. And then it was weeks before she'd agree to anything but lunch dates."

Sarah had to smother a grin. She'd known Rusty would love the challenge of an ice princess like Leslie Simmons—mostly he had to beat women off with a stick. And she'd known Leslie would be safe with Rusty, even if he managed to melt her protective facade. "I don't know, Rusty. Ultimatums. Strategy. Whatever happened to romance?"

"I don't have any more time for romance. I'm pushing thirty and I want to start a family. Even though she drives me crazy, I'm in love with Leslie Simmons. I'll do whatever it takes to make sure she's the mother of my children. And you know what they say. All's fair—"

"So everyone tells me. And what do you mean, pushing thirty? You're the same age as me. We're four years away from thirty."

"Time flies—"

"When you're having fun."

"Are we having fun?"

"Not yet."

Rusty put his arm along the back of her seat and looked over his shoulder. "From the looks of the trunk and the back seat, you had some serious fun at the mall. The Brannan girls' annual shopping spree, right? What all did you buy?"

"A little of this, a little of that." Sarah stared at the road ahead, unwilling to look him in the eye.

"Like what?" He put his face close to hers and narrowed his eyes. "Why are you blushing, Brannan?"

"Dresses," she mumbled.

"Excuse me? I thought you said dresses."

"I did. I bought dresses. At Neiman-Marcus."

"Well, well, well." He sat back and crossed his arms across his chest. "And why did you do that? I distinctly remember the night you said you'd never wear a dress again. Ninth grade. Freshman prom. Strapless dress. No boobs. First you lost your padding, then you lost your formal." He snickered.

Sarah felt the blood rush to her cheeks. She punched him in the ribs again. "No wonder Leslie wouldn't marry you. You're mean!"

Rubbing his side, Rusty grinned at her. "Aw, Sarah. I didn't mean to embarrass you. That happened years ago—and what gallant young man gave you his jacket?"

"You did. And you slugged Pete Harris for calling me flat-chested. Although he probably didn't deserve a bloody nose. It was an accurate description, at the time."

From the corner of her eye Sarah could see Rusty ogling her chest. "You outgrew it."

"Enough. What are you going to do about you and Leslie?"

"Be patient. Try and wear her down. What else can I do?" He stared out the window for a few minutes.

"What's with the dresses, Brannan? Have you finally got a love life?"

"You don't want to know. Ready to eat? We're coming into Marble Falls."

"Sounds good to me."

Once they were settled in a booth and had given the waitress their orders, Rusty persisted. "Why did you buy dresses, Sarah?"

"It's time I changed my image," she said loftily, to cover her embarrassment. "And because . . . we may not be pushing thirty, but I'm ready to settle down, too." She sighed.

"Leslie told me you had something going with what's-his-name—the head honcho at Loganetics. What happened?"

"His name is Jake Logan. In a nutshell, we're in the same boat, you and I. I want to get married. He wants us to live together."

"Son of a—" Rusty's face turned red "—gun! Want me to beat him up?"

"No, thanks. Although that might work better than Barbara and Laura's plan."

"What's their plan? Torture the poor man until he cries 'uncle'? That's the usual Brannan woman approach, right?"

"Right."

"It's a good plan. It worked for them."

"Yes, but I'm not sure I can execute it. I'm not very good at games." She took a sip of water. "What's wrong with us, Rusty? Why can't we find someone who feels like we do?"

They exchanged looks. "No." they said simultaneously.

"We tried that once—"

"It would never work—"

"On the other hand—"

"As a last resort—"

"We could have a pact. We were always good with pacts. We are blood brothers." He grabbed her left hand and rubbed his fingers across the tiny scar on her thumb.

"What kind of pact?" She turned his hand over. His scar ran from the tip of his thumb to his palm. "The blood brother one got you eight stitches and me in a heap of trouble."

"The knife slipped. It wasn't your fault. As for the pact, we could swear we'll marry each other if neither of us is hitched before we're thirty." He looked at her expectantly, his blue eyes sparkling with mischief.

Sarah tilted her head and grinned at him. She could definitely do worse. "Make it forty and it's a deal." Forty was years and years away. Plenty of time to either get Jake or get him out of her system.

"Deal. Spit."

Sarah spat in the palm of her right hand. Rusty did the same. Solemnly they shook hands.

"Eeuww! Were pacts always that nasty?" Wiping her hand on her napkin, Sarah made a face.

"Yeah. You just didn't notice it when we were kids." He rubbed his hand on his jeans. "How do you feel about our pact? Truth."

"Nothing personal, but I hope Leslie comes to her senses real soon."

"You and me both. Although, as consolation prizes go, you aren't bad." He wiggled his eyebrows at her.

"Gee, thanks."

"Now, what was it you wanted to know about men?"

Sarah leaned forward, her eyes bright. "What exactly did Leslie do to make you crazy? Tell me everything."

Jake Logan prowled his office, going from his desk at one end of the large room to the conference table at the other end. As he passed by his desk for the twenty-second time, he stopped long enough to turn on his computer and call up the E-mail file.

Still no response from Sarah. He'd sent her a message telling her to come to his office as soon as she got to work. Then he'd watched from his office window until she'd driven into the parking lot that morning. The strange muscle twitch beneath his left eye hadn't stopped until he'd seen her pull her red Toyota into its usual parking place.

Now, after waiting for Sarah for thirty minutes, he couldn't sit still, his palms were sweaty and he was grinding his teeth. With an effort, he relaxed his jaw. But he kept pacing.

Frustration—that had to be what was making him feel tense and out of control. He couldn't take much more of it. He had to get Sarah where he wanted her soon, or he'd go nuts. She was interfering with his work. His life. He couldn't think. He hadn't had one coherent, logical thought about anything for days—not since she'd so unexpectedly turned down his suggestion that they live together.

He checked his E-mail again. Still no receipt for his message. Of course, it was possible Sarah hadn't turned on her computer yet. He hit another key, and brought up the LAN file that told him who was logged into the Loganetics network. No SJB, Sarah Jane Brannan.

What was she doing? The last thing he'd told her before leaving Hamilton Friday morning was to come to his office first thing on Monday. Laura and Barbara had been hustling her into a station wagon at the time, but she'd heard him. And she'd nodded her agreement. He was almost positive of that.

Jake eyed the telephone. He'd call her, but he was almost sure she wasn't going to give him anything but a hard time on the phone. He got up and walked to the window opposite his desk. He looked down at the employee parking lot. Her red Toyota was still there. At least she hadn't come to work just to clean out her desk and leave.

He opened the door to the reception area. "Mrs. Bradshaw? Call Sarah Brannan and tell her—I mean ask her to come to my office right away. Please."

"Yes, sir." His efficient secretary reached for her telephone. Jake ducked back inside his office and sat down at his desk to wait. A few minutes later there was a brisk knock on his door.

"Come in, Sarah," he said.

The relief he felt on seeing her walk through the door vanished almost immediately. Through clenched teeth, he asked, "What have you got on?"

"A dress." She did a slow pirouette. "Like it?"

Blood thundering in his ears, Jake stared at her. The green dress clung to every curve—no, only to those curves six—no, eight inches above her knees. "That's not appropriate."

Sarah raised an eyebrow, but said nothing.

"Not only is it not appropriate, it's not decent. Take it off."

"Mr. Logan! What are you suggesting? If you called me in here to subject me to sexual harassment, I'm leaving."

He closed his eyes and silently recited the programmer's alphabet until he regained a semblance of control. "I didn't mean for you to take it off here. Go home and put on something else." He pointed at her knees. "That... violates the dress code."

"Loganetics doesn't have a dress code," she said loftily, lifting her nose in the air.

Sarah sat down and crossed her legs. Her shapely, silk clad legs. Sarah was not tall. How could she have such long legs? His gaze traveled slowly from her dainty ankles to her thighs—he jerked his head up. "I can see your thighs. No bare thighs in the workplace. That's the dress code."

"That's not true. Some of the male programmers wore shorts to work last summer. You didn't send them home to change."

"It's not summer." And hairy, male thighs didn't make him break out in a cold sweat.

Sarah recrossed her legs. The dress hiked up another inch. Jake groaned and rubbed his stomach, trying to soothe the burning he felt there. Was he getting an ulcer, on top of everything else that was going wrong with his life?

"Besides, my thighs are not bare. I have on hose. Panty hose." She looked grieved for a moment, then she focused on him, and her face brightened.

Jake couldn't stop his gaze from roaming over her. He narrowed his eyes. "Are you wearing underwear?"

Her mouth dropped open. "What kind of question is that?"

"You're not wearing underwear, are you?"

"It's really none of your business." A gleam appeared in her green eyes, one he'd never seen there before. Her lush lips curved into a wicked, un-Sarah-like smile. "If you must know, I'm not wearing panties. The way this wool jersey clings, if I wore panties there would be a panty line. But I do have on—"

"Stop!" Making a strangled sound, Jake held up his hand like a traffic cop. "I don't want to hear any more about your—what you are or are not wearing."

"A bra." Shrugging, Sarah sat back in her chair. "You asked."

"Panties—" He cleared his throat. "Underwear is required for everyone. That is definitely part of the dress code. You'll have to go home and change. Put on those gray slacks, the ones you wear with the dark green sweater. That sweater makes your eyes look like emeralds. Just like the dress."

"Emeralds? Why, Jake, that's so poetic. I never knew you thought my eyes looked like jewels. I never even knew you paid attention to what I was wearing."

"Is that why you wore a dress? So I'd notice you?"

"Sort of. I wore it so I'd get noticed. But not by you. I've given up on you." She gave him a brave smile. "But no hard feelings. You are the boss, and I suppose you have a right to know why I decided to come back to work. Even though you and I are, you know, finished. The truth is, I'm husband hunting. Did you know that most romances start in the workplace? I read it in *Cosmopolitan.*'' She frowned. ''Or maybe it was *Newsweek.* Anyway, Loganetics is as good a workplace as any, better than some. All the engineers and programmers, not to mention the accountants and the legal staff—''

''Husband hunting!'' he roared. A red haze appeared in front of his eyes. The pulse pounding in his ears grew louder.

''That's right.'' She stood up and smoothed the dress over her hips, then did another slow turn. When she was facing him again, she said archly, ''The dress is my way of advertising. What do you think? Will it do the trick?''

The red haze turned crimson. Sarah Brannan was going to use his company to hunt for a husband? Not on her life—but maybe on his. Seeing her like this just might kill him if he didn't do something fast. Could the strange clutching feeling in his chest mean he was having a heart attack? Jake stood and moved around the desk.

He had things to do before he died.

Sarah backed up. ''Wh-what's wrong? Jake, what are you going to do?''

As he advanced on her, he made his plan. He was good at planning. First, he was going to kiss her senseless, then he would take that sexy dress off her, lay her on the conference table and—

''Jake!''

He stopped in his tracks. Sarah had backed up against the table. Now she looked downright scared. Jake shook his head to clear it, then looked into her startled green eyes. He took a deep, shuddering breath and struggled for control. His brain was trying to send him a message, an important one, about something he'd heard recently.

He drew his brows together in fierce concentration. What was it Colt had said? Something about sexy dresses—dresses no decent woman would wear in public. Yeah, that was it. Barbara and Laura had worn dresses like this when they were sneaking up on Vince and Colt. Jake let his breath out in a satisfied whoosh. Now that he understood what was happening, he could relax. He wasn't having a heart attack.

Sarah was coming on to him.

He grinned at her. "On second thought, the dress looks great on you. How about lunch?"

Moving away from the conference table, she gave him a confused glance, then looked at the clock on the wall behind his desk. "It's not even ten o'clock yet."

"Not now. At one. I'll come by for you."

Sarah inched toward the door to his office. She had gone from scared to wary, but she obviously didn't trust him. That made his heart constrict painfully again. "Please, Sarah?" he asked humbly.

"No. I am not going out with you."

It might only have been wishful thinking on his part, but her refusal didn't sound as forceful as it might have. "We need to talk about that. And we don't have to go out. We can order in. Okay?"

"No. I am not going out or staying in with you."

"It's only lunch," he coaxed.

She took a deep breath, then said in a rush of words, "No, I can't go to lunch with you. There's no point, and besides, I have a previous engagement."

"With who?" he asked through clenched teeth. He could feel his body tensing up again.

"With whom."

"Who. Whom. Who cares? What's his name?"

Her chin came up. "None of your business." She headed for the door.

Jake followed. She was trying to make him jealous, that was all. No doubt another trick she'd learned from her sisters. So she was having lunch with another man. Big deal. What could happen in an hour?

The burning sensation returned, this time in his gut. A lot could happen in an hour. In that dress, a lot could happen in ten minutes. "Dinner, then. Seven o'clock? We can go to that new Mexican place on Sixth Avenue."

"No."

Jake frowned. She was not making things easy for him. But he'd find a way to get back in her good graces. He had to. Life without the possibility of an affair with Sarah was too painful to contemplate. He looked at her more closely. That strange glitter was back in her eyes. The little minx was playing games with him.

Jake smothered a grin. Didn't she know he'd made his first million designing computer games? He was a master player. No way was a little country girl like Sarah Brannan going to outmaneuver him. She wasn't in his league.

He shoved his fingers through his hair and gave Sarah his best mournful look. "No lunch, no dinner? When will I see you again?" He moved closer. "I need to see you, Sarah," he whispered huskily.

"Why? I want to get married. You don't. You are no longer on my list of eligibles. We kissed goodbye, remember?"

"No." He was only inches away from her now. This time she was standing her ground, although her hand hovered nervously over the doorknob. Encouraged, he put his hands on her waist and held her loosely. "I don't remember. Maybe we should do it again."

Her voice faint, Sarah said, "Only one goodbye kiss per customer. That's a rule."

"A rule made to be broken, if I ever heard one." Jake lowered his head and touched her lips with his. Go slow, he told himself. He didn't want her to panic again.

Sarah's lips softened beneath his, and he increased the pressure. Her lips parted and he deepened the kiss, taking possession of her mouth with all the skill he could muster. He had to drive the thought of any other man right out of her head.

Moving one hand from her waist to the nape of her neck, he held her in place, wrapping his other arm more tightly around her, pulling her into the heated cradle of his thighs. She was melting against him, molding her body to his and allowing him access to every secret her mouth held. She was kissing him back, and making soft, purring noises deep in her throat. He wanted more, as much as she was willing to give, but this was not the time or place.

Reluctantly, he ended the kiss. He managed to keep enough of his wits about him to murmur, "Goodbye, Sarah."

Sarah touched her fingertips to her mouth. "Goodbye?" she asked, blinking her eyes.

She appeared to be dazed. Knowing he could affect her almost as much as she affected him made his heart swell with some unidentifiable emotion—pride, maybe. His voice husky, he told her, "For now. I have a company to run."

Putting his hand in the small of her back, he pushed her gently out the door.

Chapter Five

Sarah leaned against the door to Jake's office, sure her wobbly knees would not carry her one step farther. Thank goodness she'd made it out the door before losing control of her motor functions.

Mrs. Bradshaw, Jake's grandmotherly secretary, half rose from her desk. "Are you all right, dear? You look faint. Did that man do something to you?"

Pushing herself away from the door, Sarah motioned for Mrs. Bradshaw to remain seated. "No, no. I'm okay. Jake—Mr. Logan didn't do anything." Except take her breath away and turn her bones to jelly. How was she ever going to resist him long enough to make him realize they belonged together forever?

"Well, if you're sure..." Mrs. Bradshaw said dubiously. "He's been in such a strange mood lately. I've never seen him like this."

Sarah perked up. That was promising, assuming she, and not an overdose of turkey, was the cause. "Like how?"

"Like almost human. You know how he is—logical, imperturbable, always in control. Mr. Logan would never let on if anything was bothering him, until recently. Now he's moody, even downright rude at times." Mrs. Bradshaw drew herself even more upright—the picture of offended sensibility.

Sarah made a sympathetic noise.

"Oh, he always apologizes right away, but it's just not like him to be so...emotional. Not only that—he can't seem to make even the simplest decision. He'll ask for something, then two seconds later, he'll tell me to forget it. If I didn't know better, I'd think..."

"What?"

"He might be coming down with something. But he's never been sick one day since I started working for him. And that was almost ten years ago. Whatever is going on, I hope it's over soon. I retire in three months, and I'm too old to adjust to a new boss, even if he is an improved version, in some ways."

Walking back to her office, Sarah tried to figure out who had won the first skirmish in her and Jake's private little war between the sexes. Once she got to her desk, she spent a good twenty minutes reliving every minute of the encounter.

In her favor, he had reacted to the dress just the way Barbara had predicted; his eyes had bugged out and he'd turned an odd shade of purple. Telling him she was husband hunting—her very own contribution to the Brannan sisters' plan—had worked well, too. Especially when she'd followed through by refusing to tell him who—with whom—she was lunching. If he'd known her lunch date was with Leslie Simmons, he wouldn't have been nearly as upset.

Sarah picked up a pencil and tapped the eraser on the edge of her desk. "Upset" wasn't the right word. He'd been jealous, possessive and a little crazy. Just the way her sisters had predicted he'd be, and just the way she wanted him. She grinned, twirling the pencil like a miniature baton. It had been worth even the aggravation of panty hose to see him like that. The plan was working.

Dropping the pencil on the desk, Sarah leaned back in her chair and smiled. Yes, everything had gone her way, until—

She sat up abruptly, her smile drooping into a frown. Until Jake had kissed her. One touch of his sexy mouth on hers and she'd forgotten all about strategy and tactics. When he had begun working his magic with his lips, she hadn't been able to do anything but respond. Keeping her mind on the plan had been impossible.

Her sisters had told her thwarting a man's every move was the Brannan woman's tried-and-true method of turning a would-be seducer into a fiancé.

They hadn't said how hard it would be.

Why had she ever thought she could make the plan work? She'd never been any good at games. Sarah had a sudden, panicky feeling that playing silly games wasn't going to get her anything but big trouble and a broken heart.

She took several deep breaths and concentrated on the positive. Jake *had* kissed her. He had said it was a goodbye kiss, but he hadn't meant that, any more than she had meant it when she'd kissed him goodbye in the bathroom. He might have kissed her to get even with her for teasing him with the dress. But the kiss hadn't seemed like retribution, more like slow, delicious torture.

No, Jake had been showing her exactly what she was missing by holding out for a wedding ring. That was ironic, since she'd been demonstrating what he was missing by not walking down the aisle.

All of a sudden, Granny Brannan's favorite exhortation echoed in her mind. "Show some spunk, young lady!" Sarah stiffened her spine. What was she? A Brannan woman or a wimp? This contest was *not* going to end in a tie! She would never win if she panicked at the first sign of trouble. And she had to win. If Jake won they'd both be losers.

The telephone rang.

Sarah started guiltily. She'd been at work for hours, and she hadn't even turned on her computer yet. She picked up the receiver. "Hello."

Mrs. Bradshaw's voice came over the line. "Hello, Sarah. Mr. Logan asked me to call. He wants you to get ready for a business trip right away. The beta tests on the time management program are beginning tomorrow."

"Business trip? I don't understand. I never go on trips." Something else wasn't right about Mrs. Bradshaw's statement, but Sarah was so surprised she could grasp only one fact—Jake was sending her away. Her heart sank. It had been a goodbye kiss, after all.

"You'll need the TimeMaster files and clothes for a week, he said. He wants you to see how the test is set up and run."

"Wait a minute. Tomorrow can't be right. I'm sure the tests weren't scheduled to begin until next year."

"Apparently, there's been a change in plans." Mrs. Bradshaw lowered her voice. "Remember what I told you about the way Mr. Logan's been acting lately? This is another example."

"I can't go anywhere right now," Sarah protested. She had to be in the same city if she was going to entice, entrance and ultimately entrap Jake. "Let me talk to Mr. Logan."

"I'm sorry, dear. He's not available. He's meeting with the engineers and programmers. But you can talk to him later today. He said he'll pick you up at your apartment in two hours."

"Jake is picking me up? Personally?"

"Yes. At noon. At your apartment."

"Oh. Well, then. I guess I'd better go home and pack." At least he was going to drive her to the airport. She'd have a chance to tell him what she thought about him running her out of town at the first opportunity. Jake Logan was a coward.

With a toss of her head, Sarah loaded the Time-Master files in her tote bag and drove home. Once there, she packed quickly. Her usual wardrobe went into the suitcase—she wasn't wasting her new dresses on engineers and programmers. Then she waited impatiently for Jake to arrive. She was looking forward to letting him know he was only getting a temporary reprieve.

He might need a few days to adjust to the new Sarah. She'd give him that. But if he was counting on "out of sight, out of mind," she was placing her faith in "absence makes the heart grow fonder." Either way, she'd be back, and sooner or later Jake would realize what he felt for her was more than lust. Her mission was to hang in there until the light of true love shining from her eyes was reflected in his. Persistence had paid off for Laura and Barbara, and she could be just as tenacious as her sisters.

A black Jaguar pulled up and parked next to her Toyota. Jake got out and started up her walk. Sarah opened the door of her garden apartment, not waiting for his knock.

"Hello, Sarah." He took her bags and briefcase and put them in the trunk of the car. He looked her up and down, then gave a satisfied nod. She was wearing gray slacks and her favorite green sweater. "I see you took my advice, and changed into something more appropriate for work."

"I changed clothes because—" She swallowed the rest of her explanation. She didn't want to admit that she'd changed clothes for him, but maybe she had. Why else would she have chosen the sweater he'd said made her eyes sparkle like jewels? She had a sinking feeling—she should have stayed in her game clothes.

"Yes?" He opened the passenger door.

"I wanted to be comfortable on the flight to Dallas." Sarah took her seat and waited until Jake was behind the wheel.

Jake started the engine and backed into the street. "Dallas? We're not going to Dallas."

"I beg your pardon. Mrs. Bradshaw said the beta tests for TimeMaster were starting. Those tests are in Dallas, at that big insurance company. Aren't they?"

"That test isn't scheduled until after Christmas. I thought you knew that. This is a preliminary test, on a smaller scale."

"Where am I going, then?"

"We're going to San Antonio."

"You're going, too?"

"Yes."

"Why are you going? Don't you have employees to do this sort of thing?"

He nodded. "Of course, but I've been trapped behind a desk too long. I need to do this, to remind myself what Loganetics is really all about. Plus, I promised Colt I'd handle everything personally." He paused long enough to send her a smoldering glance. "And I wanted to keep an eye on you."

The way he looked at her made her tingle all over, but Sarah made herself focus on his second reason. "Colt? Colt McCauley, my brother-in-law?"

"That's the one. I talked to him last Friday, and he agreed to let us use his law office as a test site. If TimeMaster does what it's designed to do, he should be able to spend a lot more hours with his wife and children."

Sarah's heart lurched. "You're letting Colt test TimeMaster?" Loganetics always used its largest customers for test sites. Marketing strategy, Jake said. The customer was more likely to buy a product they'd had a hand in developing. But an office the size of Colt's would never need more than one or two programs. "Why?" she asked softly.

"Why not?" Jake responded, his voice gruff. "He needs time. We can give it to him." As he merged with the traffic on Interstate 35 South, he asked, "Do you want to stop for lunch before we leave Austin, or wait until we get to San Antonio? We should be at the hotel in an hour or so."

"Lunch. Oh my gosh. I forgot to call—"

"And cancel your appointment? No problem. Use the car phone."

Sarah narrowed her eyes. Jake might be doing Colt a very big favor, but he also had a less altruistic motive—to get her where he wanted her, in his bed. He was playing his own game, and he was using her family to do it. He was sneaky enough to be a Brannan, no doubt about it. She dialed Loganetics. "Extension 324, please."

Jake's knuckles whitened as he tightened his grip on the steering wheel. He must have recognized the number as one of the programmers' extensions. If she could make him continue to believe she'd had a lunch date with a man, she'd be ahead in the game. Sarah breathed a sigh of relief when Leslie answered the phone. Her secret would have been out if she'd had to ask for her by name.

"Hi. It's me. I called to tell you I won't be able to go to lunch with you, after all. I'm on my way to San Antonio." She listened while Leslie asked if she'd been assigned to the sudden TimeMaster beta tests. "That's right, I'm going along to observe. It should help make the manual more useful. I'll call you when I get back." She could see Jake's scowl reflected in the rearview mirror. "Bye, Les—"

Sarah gnashed her teeth. Double darn. Putting the cellular phone back in its cradle, she looked out the side window. Maybe Jake hadn't caught her slip.

"Les. Now who would that be?," he mused. "I don't know any programmer named Les." Jake drummed his fingers on the steering wheel for a second or two. "Aha! You were talking to Leslie Simmons. You were having lunch with her, not another man."

Disgruntled, Sarah said, "I never said I was."

"You wanted me to think you were—admit it. That talk about husband hunting was a ploy to make me jealous."

Coolly, she raised her eyebrow. "Why would I want to do that? Jealous or not, you're out of the running. I thought Leslie might know someone she could fix me up with. That article I read said one of the best ways to meet prospective partners was through friends. I need all the help I can get. You know what they say—a good man is hard to find."

He patted her on the knee. "You don't have to look any farther. I'm right here." He left his hand on her knee.

She picked up his hand with two fingers and put it back on the steering wheel. Dusting her fingers together, she told him haughtily, "You're not my type."

He chuckled. "Yes, I am. Did Mrs. Bradshaw tell you we will be staying at the Casa del Rio? Colt said his office wasn't far from there."

"No, she didn't even tell me we were going to San Antonio, remember? Where are all the computers and equipment? They can't be in the trunk of this car."

"The engineers are bringing the hardware to set up the LAN. The programmer has the software. I have you."

"Only for business, and not for long." She gave him a suspicious look. "You haven't done anything underhanded and sneaky, like putting us in the same room, have you?"

"At a fine old establishment like the Casa del Rio? They'd never allow an unmarried couple to share a room."

"Does that mean you asked?" she asked sweetly.

"No, it means we're in a suite."

She shot him her best quelling glance. "I'll stay with Laura and Colt."

He laughed out loud. "I was joking, Sarah. You have a room all to yourself." He turned a serious face to her. "This is a business trip, first and foremost. The rest of the staff will be at the hotel, and I want you there, too. We may have some late-night meetings."

He sounded more like a boss than a lover, so Sarah decided to believe him. "All right. I'll stay at the hotel. But if we have any free evenings, I want to spend them with my family."

"Of course. As a matter of fact, Colt invited me to dinner at his home tonight. Why don't you come along?"

"I'll think about it."

They stopped for lunch at a German restaurant in New Braunfels, and arrived at the hotel around two. Sarah wandered around the lobby while Jake checked them in and left messages for the other Loganetics employees. She was staring at a display of resort wear in the lobby boutique when Jake joined her. The mannequin was wearing a thong bikini.

Jake gave it no more than a cursory glance, then turned all his attention to her. He escorted her to the elevator, and pushed the button for the fifth floor. When they arrived, he gave her the key to room 508.

"Get settled and think about what you'd like to do this afternoon. The other members of the team won't be arriving until this evening, so we have until then to play tourists. When you're ready to go out, give me a call. I'm in room 510."

Sarah stopped in the act of turning the key in the lock. "This evening? The others aren't arriving until this evening? Then why are we here so early?"

"I had my reasons."

She eyed him warily. "What reasons?"

"Never mind about that. Unpack, and give me a call." He pushed her gently through her door and closed it before she could finish.

As soon as she was alone in her room, Sarah decided not to worry about Jake's mysterious reasons for getting them to San Antonio before the rest of the team. It meant Jake wanted to be with her—that was good. And he was doing nice things for her family. Things were definitely looking up. She flopped on the bed, and picked up the telephone. She had to call Laura and confer.

"Hi, Sarah. Colt told me about the computer system Jake is installing in his office. He also said you and Jake will be joining us for dinner. What's going on? How did you manage to get the boss to bring you along on a business trip?"

"It wasn't my idea—he ordered me to come. Jake is up to something. And I'm not sure what."

"Tell me everything."

Sarah did, beginning with Jake's reaction to seeing her in a dress, and ending with the unexpected trip to San Antonio.

"Hmm. He's smart, very smart. You see what he's done, of course. He asked you to lunch and dinner. You turned him down."

"That's what I was supposed to do."

"That's not the point. Who did you have lunch with?"

"Jake."

"Who are you dining with?"

"Jake."

"Are you wearing a dress?"

Sarah made a face. "No, darn it. I knew it was a mistake to change. If I'd kept the dress on, I'd have at least one with me. As it is, I have none. I changed because I thought I wasn't going to see Jake for a week. And the panty hose were killing me."

Laura made a clucking sound. "You've got to learn to suffer if you want to win."

Sarah opened her mouth, then closed it. What could she say? She wasn't doing so well, after all. Jake Logan had gotten everything he wanted. She'd had lunch with him, and he expected her to spend the afternoon in his company, as well as dine with him. Her dresses were still in their plastic bags, back in Austin. "I guess I lost this round, didn't I?"

"A minor setback," Laura said airily. "You'll win the next one. Jake is a real challenge, all right. The good ones always are. But we'll get him in the end, just wait and see."

"Aren't there any rules in this game?" Sarah wailed.

"All's fair—"

"So everyone keeps telling me. But I didn't think cheating was allowed. Jake cheats. He had the trip to San Antonio planned since Friday. He knew all along that we'd be together for a whole week. He let me think—never mind. What are we going to do now?"

"Go buy another dress, for starters. We'll talk more tonight. And Sarah, if you really love Jake and you're sure he loves you, then lose those scruples. Cheat back."

Sarah hung up the telephone. Before she could cheat, she had to get back in the game. But how? Another dress wasn't the answer. Jake had reacted nicely the first time, but now that he knew what to expect he'd be ready for her.

She had to do something unexpected.

The bikini in the boutique flashed into her mind. Did she dare? Would he care?

"Faint heart never won fair knight." An almost bare bottom would certainly get his attention. And no one else's, if she were lucky. Playing games was one thing. Being the spectacle in a spectator sport was another. Hopefully, the hotel pool would not be crowded on a Monday afternoon.

Minutes later, Sarah was back in her room in front of the mirrored closet door, twisting around to see her backside. "This really is indecent," she muttered. But she needed something outrageous to get his attention again. "But if this doesn't work, I'm giving up on Brannan tactics."

The phone rang. It was Jake. "Hi. What are you up to?"

Before she could change her mind, Sarah said boldly, "I'm going swimming."

"Swimming?"

He sounded surprised. Good. Off-balance was the way she wanted him. "Is that all right with you?" she asked demurely. "I thought we weren't starting the job until tomorrow morning. And I talked to Laura—dinner's not until seven."

"Yeah, that's right. But I was hoping we could do something together this afternoon..."

His voice was low and husky and she could hear him breathing. She couldn't let his sexy voice affect her equilibrium—if she fell at his feet now, it would be a mistake. Sarah straightened her back, but that didn't stop the tiny chills creeping up and down her spine.

"Together? What did you have in mind?" she asked, intentionally making her voice husky. He should have a few chills, too.

"I could come to your room, and continue where I left off this morning. Remember?"

"Of course I remember. You kissed me goodbye."

"Only for the moment. Now I want to kiss you hello. More than once, and not just on the mouth. That place just beneath your ear, the nape of your neck... There are other places...."

He trailed off. The chills stopped. Now she felt hot all over. Fanning herself with her hand, she told herself a dip in the pool would take care of that. Until then, she had to sound cool, at least. Forcing ice into her voice, she told him, "You said this was first and foremost a business trip. Spending the afternoon...doing what you said doesn't sound like a business meeting to me."

"Business starts first thing tomorrow. But if you don't want to kiss me, we could visit the Alamo. It's just across the street. I hear the Daughters of the Texas Revolution conduct very nice tours."

"I've seen the Alamo. I'm going swimming."

"I can't go swimming. I didn't bring a suit."

"Neither did I. I bought one at that shop in the lobby—the one that was in the window. You could get one, too."

There was a pause. A long pause. "You bought a bikini?" He sounded as if someone was strangling him.

"That's right. In red. With a gauzy kind of cover-up, and I got some red plastic sandals, too. Very trendy. Just the thing to attract Mr. Right."

"Sarah. You listen to me. Stay where you are. I'll be there in a minute. I'm just next door. Don't you leave your room until—"

She hung up on him.

"Sarah!" Jake slammed the telephone down and headed for the door. He made it to the hall in time to see a flash of red disappearing into an elevator. Looking around wildly, he spotted a maid coming out of a room. "Where's the swimming pool?"

"On the roof. Take the elevator to the tenth floor."

Jake stabbed the button for the elevator and waited impatiently. A thong bikini? What in the hell was Sarah thinking of? The elevator doors opened slowly, revealing an interior crowded with a bellhop, a family of four and enough luggage for a trip around the world. Jake shoved in anyway. He was on the opposite side from the buttons. "Tenth floor."

When the outraged woman scrunched in the corner glared at him, he added, "Please."

The family got off at the seventh floor.

Jake stepped into the tenth floor hall and looked around. An arrow pointed to the exercise room and swimming pool. He followed the trail to a door leading to a glass-enclosed heated pool.

Sarah was standing just inside the door. She was wearing the bikini, partially concealed by a shirtlike affair that ended well above her knees—a cover-up she'd called it. It didn't cover nearly enough. The gauzy stuff allowed him to see the tantalizing shape of her derriere. Him, and everyone else present.

A balding businessman with a paunch that hung over his baggy swimsuit was sitting on the edge of the pool, dangling his feet in the water. A muscular blond giant stood on the end of the diving board. Both men were watching Sarah like patrons at a sleazy strip joint.

Neither man paid any attention to Jake, not even when he made a growling noise deep in his throat.

Sarah heard him, though. She turned around. "Jake!"

She stood stiffly, clutching a towel to her chest and staring at him. For a scant moment, Sarah looked as though she might be regretting her impulsive purchase. Then she raised an eyebrow and dropped the towel.

"I see you decided to join me. But where's your swimsuit?"

"I'm not going swimming and neither are you."

She took a step backward. "Oh, yes I am." She began to shrug out of the shirt.

"Not a chance, Sarah. No one is going to see your naked tush but me."

The cover-up floated to the ground. The sight of Sarah's breasts, barely covered by two scraps of red material, distracted him momentarily—long enough for her to turn around and move to the edge of the pool. Jake took a quick step forward, intending to seize her before she dived into the water. His frantic grab missed, and he slipped on the wet ceramic tiles, bumping against Sarah.

Waving her arms wildly, Sarah fell into the pool. Jake's forward momentum sent him in after her.

He came up out of the water, sputtering and choking.

Dashing the water out of his eyes, he looked for Sarah. She was treading water a few feet away from him, and eyeing him warily. "Do you always swim in a business suit?"

"No. I don't know how to sw—" Jake sank beneath the surface again.

"Jake! I'll save you!"

Keeping his face underwater, Jake smiled. She'd fallen for it. He let his body go limp the minute he felt her touch. She grabbed him by the hair and jerked his head out of the water.

"Owww! Watch it, Sarah—"

It wasn't Sarah. The blond giant transferred his grip from Jake's hair to around his neck. Within moments, he'd hoisted Jake out of the pool. As Jake lay on the cool tiles, struggling for breath, the he-man turned his attention to Sarah, holding out his hand to her.

Jake managed to stand as Sarah put her hand in the blonde's and let him pull her out of the pool.

"Cover yourself," he gasped, looking around for her shirt. "Do you want to be arrested for indecent exposure?"

"Jake! You should at least thank the man for saving your life. Why didn't you tell me you can't swim?"

"I can swim," he mumbled, shaking hands with the giant. "Thanks, anyway." Then he sneezed violently, three times.

"Are you all right?" She grabbed a towel from a stack on a table and began drying his hair and face. "You'd better go back to your room and get out of these wet clothes. The water was warm, so I don't think you'll catch pneumonia or anything, but you look ridiculous."

He took the towel away from her and wrapped it around her waist. "Don't worry about how I'm dressed. You'd better get into more clothes before you catch hell."

"Jake, you're overreacting. What I'm wearing is perfectly acceptable."

"Yeah, right." He picked up her cover-up and began shoving her arms into the sleeves. "At the nude beaches in Cannes, maybe. But we're not in France." He sneezed again.

"Let's get you back to your room."

Dripping and squishing, they got in an empty elevator. Sarah pushed the button for the fifth floor.

They made it to seven before the elevator stopped. The door opened and the same family that he'd ridden up with joined them on the elevator. One of the little girls tugged on her mother's hand. "Mommy, why is that man all wet?"

The woman looked him up and down. Jake bristled when her husband did the same to Sarah. Shoving her behind him, he snarled, "I had to jump in the pool to save her."

"My hero!" said Sarah admiringly. Then she spoiled it by snickering.

As soon as they exited the elevator, Jake took her by the arm and dragged her down the hall. He let her go at her door. "Get dressed and we'll talk."

"What about? I'm not in the mood for a lecture."

"Too bad. You're going to get one. You crossed the line this time, Sarah. Those men were leering at you." He stood in front of the door to his room, and fumbled in his pockets, looking for his room key.

"Those weren't leers. They were admiring glances." Sarah took her key from the pocket of her cover-up and inserted it in the lock.

"Get this straight, Sarah. As long as you belong to me, you will not flaunt your delectable little body in front of other men."

"I don't belong to you." She opened her door. "Delectable, hmm? That's interesting."

"I'm not going to argue with you."

"About being delectable? I knew you didn't mean that. You think I'm too round."

"Your shape is fine. And it's all mine. The sooner you admit it, the better."

She winked at him as she began closing the door. "I thought you weren't going to argue."

He put his hand up to keep the door from closing completely. "Wait. I don't have my key. I must have left it in the room."

"Come in, then. I'll call the front desk and have them send up another one."

As soon as he entered, she pushed him toward the bathroom. "Stand in there, so you won't drip all over the carpet." She was laughing at him again.

He'd show her a thing or two. He waited until she had her back turned, dialing the front desk, then peeled off his jacket. It hit the floor with a soggy plop. His shirt followed.

Sarah looked over her shoulder. Her eyes widened. "Hello, front desk? Mr. Logan locked his key in his room. Could you send a key for room 510 to room 508? Thanks." She hung up the telephone just as he was stripping off his wet pants. "What are you doing?" she said, looking him up and down.

Jake grinned as she tried unsuccessfully to keep her gaze on his face. Knowing Sarah couldn't resist giving him the once-over gave his ego just the boost it needed. "You told me to get out of these wet clothes."

Sarah turned her back, but not before he saw her face go pink. "I didn't mean for you to do it here."

"What's wrong, Sarah? If I was wearing a bathing suit you wouldn't be embarrassed."

"That's not a swimsuit. It's your underwear." Sarah sounded shocked. She wasn't nearly as sophisticated as a woman who wore a thong bikini should be.

"So what? At least my buns are covered." He sneezed again, and a chill went through him. Time to stop teasing Sarah and get warm, he decided reluctantly. "I think I'd better get in a hot shower. You don't mind if I use yours, do you?" He closed the bathroom door, then opened it a crack. "I can't go to my room in my underwear. As soon as the bellman brings the key, go get me some dry clothes."

She walked to the bathroom door. "You sure are bossy."

"That's because I am the boss. You better get out of your wet clothes, too."

She gave him a wicked smile. "Not just yet. I'm going for another swim."

NO POSTAGE
NECESSARY
IF MAILED
IN THE
UNITED STATES

Chapter Six

On Sunday afternoon, Sarah waved goodbye to Laura, Colt and the twins and settled back in the passenger seat of Jake's Jaguar for the return trip to Austin.

"They certainly are the picture of a happy family again." She felt a lump forming in her throat. After a week of working closely with Jake, she was more in love than ever. And she had no idea how the Brannan strategy was working. On the other hand, Jake's tactics, if that was what they were, were doing just fine.

She'd imagined from the first time she'd seen him that he was perfect husband and father material. Now she was positive she'd been right. Families obviously meant a lot to Jake. That was important. A man would have to have a strong affinity for family life to fit in with the Brannan clan.

"You have a lot to do with that," she told him.

"Me?" He shot her a surprised glance before returning his gaze to the road. "I didn't do anything."

Her heart swelled. He was modest, too. "Only automate Colt's office so he'd have more time for Laura and the kids."

"I didn't do it for them. The beta test on Loganetics TimeMaster is strictly business."

Sarah raised an eyebrow. "Oh, yeah? So tell me, how did baby-sitting the twins with me so Laura and Colt could have a romantic weekend in Galveston help the bottom line?"

"I wanted to see how kids today interact with computer games. I started Loganetics with a game, but we've gotten away from that market over the years. It may be time to get back in."

"Oh, that's why you played Nintendo with Ricky and Nicky every chance you got. The twins are nothing but guinea pigs for Loganetics. Just like Colt."

Jake's only response was a hacking cough.

Sarah winced. She'd tried to avoid thinking about what his bloodshot eyes and gray complexion meant. "Are you sure you don't want me to drive?"

Jake nodded.

"You're sick. Pull over and let me drive."

"I am not sick. I never get sick." He sneezed three times. "But if I am, it's your fault. If you hadn't made me take that impromptu swim—"

"I didn't push you in the pool. You pushed me. Besides, you don't catch cold from getting a chill." She reached over and touched his forehead. "I think you may have a fever."

Jake leaned his head into her hand momentarily, then jerked away. "No, I do not have a fever. I refuse to have a fever. But, like I said, if I do have a fever it is your fault. Everyone knows hotel swimming pools are breeding grounds for viruses. If you hadn't bought that bikini—"

"Stop! I don't want to hear another word about the bikini. It is not my fault that you're sick. You probably caught the mystery virus at Loganetics before we left."

"Maybe." He coughed again.

"You should have gone back to Austin on Friday. I told you so."

"I know. You tried very hard to get rid of me."

"I was trying to take care of you, not get rid of you. You needed rest."

He glanced over at her, a startled look in his eyes. "Take care of me? Why would you do that? I can take care of myself. I always have."

Sarah sat back and folded her arms across her chest. "And you have been doing a wonderful job. Not!"

"What does that mean?"

"It means grown men who are under the weather do not ride every ride at Fiesta Texas—after touring the zoo and the Alamo—thereby aggravating a cold by getting themselves overtired, then insist on driving ninety miles, just to prove they are not sick."

"They don't?"

"No, they don't. Jake—"

Jake turned the wheel suddenly, sending Sarah against the passenger door. He coasted into a rest area, parked the car and got out. Walking around to the passenger door, he said, "Okay, you can drive."

Sarah scooted over the gearshift to the driver's seat.

As he took her place in the passenger seat, he asked, "You have driven a Jag before, haven't you?"

"No. But I've driven everything else, from tractors to pickup trucks. How different can it be?"

"How different—" He put his face in his hands and groaned. "This is a delicate machine, not a John Deere. I'll drive."

Sarah started the engine and shifted into first gear before Jake could get out of the car. "Put on your seat belt. Here we go."

Once they were on the highway and Sarah was sure she could handle the automobile, she told him, "You'd better see a doctor the minute we get back to Austin."

"On Sunday? I don't think so."

"Call Dr. Johnson. What good is having a company doctor if you can't call him on Sunday?"

"I don't need a doctor. I feel fine." He sneezed again.

"You are the most stubborn man I've ever met." She reached into her purse and pulled out a package of tissues. "Here."

He took one and blew his nose noisily. "Thanks. Will you go out to dinner with me tonight?"

"No. You belong in bed."

"Okay. Will you join me?" His wicked chuckle turned into another cough.

"See. I told you so. You're in no condition to go out. Or to take someone to bed."

"With a little encouragement, I know I could—" he coughed "—rise to the occasion."

Sarah attempted an outraged stare, but she couldn't manage it, not with Jake looking so forlorn. She laughed instead. "You don't have to do that. Not for me."

"I wouldn't do it for anyone else. You're the only one I want."

Swallowing the lump that had returned to her throat, Sarah changed the subject. "Even if you were only motivated by crass commercialism, you were very good with the twins. Do you have younger brothers and sisters?"

"No. I'm an only child."

"Didn't either of your parents remarry after their divorce?"

Jake's laugh had a bitter edge. "Oh, yeah. They both remarried, but I don't have any brothers or sisters. My parents never were that interested in children."

"Too bad. I like large families. Do you?"

From the corner of her eye she saw him shrug. "I never thought much about it."

"Why not?"

"No need, since I don't plan to have one." He stared at the road ahead, his expression grim.

It didn't take a genius to see the dead end on that road. Still, she needed to find out exactly why Jake was so opposed to marriage for himself. He'd shown the same fascination with family life this week as he had when she'd first regaled him with stories about the Brannans.

There had to be a reason for his fascination/repulsion reaction to love and marriage. She tried another route.

"Ricky and Nicky thought you were great. Even though you didn't let them win every game. You'll make a wonderful father."

"That's something I'll never know."

"Why not? Don't you want children of your own?"

"No. I told you. I'm not interested in being part of a family."

"I don't believe you. You're too intrigued by my family, and you do too much for your employees' families—free day care, paid maternity and paternity leave. Why?"

"Benefits like that are good for business. Loganetics has a very low turnover."

"That can't be the only reason. What's the point of building a successful business if you have no one to share it with, no one to leave it to?"

"Is that why you want to marry me? You have visions of being a wealthy widow?"

Sarah clutched the steering wheel and drew in a deep breath. She felt as if she'd been kicked in the stomach.

Jake reached over and touched her cheek. "I am sorry. That was uncalled-for."

"Yes, it was." Couldn't he tell the difference between love and greed, for heaven's sake?

"I've never met a woman less interested in money." When she didn't respond, he asked, "Sarah? Forgive me?"

"All right." She shouldn't have pushed him, not when she knew he wasn't feeling well. Someday he'd tell her why he shied away from commitment. "You sound like you're about to lose your voice. Maybe you shouldn't talk anymore."

"That's a tactful way to tell me to shut up. And you're right. My throat does feel a little scratchy." He leaned his head against the headrest and closed his eyes.

The rest of the trip was silent, except for an occasional wheezing cough from Jake. When they'd arrived at her apartment and unloaded her luggage, she asked, "Do you want to come in and call Dr. Johnson from here?"

"No, thanks." He took the keys from her fingers and gave her a rheumy smile as he pulled away from the curb. She waved goodbye, a little disconcerted by his rapid departure. He hadn't tried to pressure her into going out to dinner with him, and it wasn't like him to take no for an answer so readily. He must feel really bad. She hoped Jake had enough sense to take some aspirin and go to bed, even if he didn't call the doctor.

When she entered her living room, Sarah noticed the light on her answering machine was flashing. The counter indicated she had three messages. She pushed the button to retrieve them.

Message one: "Hi, Sarah. It's me, Rusty. I need to talk to you. It's real important." He left a number Sarah recognized as his office number.

Message two: "Sarah. Rusty. Call me at work. Urgent."

Message three: "Where in the hell are you? I need you."

Sarah dialed the number of the UT Athletic Department, but there was no answer. She was looking up Leslie's number in her address book when the telephone rang. It was Rusty.

"Finally. Where have you been all week?"

"In San Antonio, working. What's wrong?"

"Leslie kicked me out."

"She took you up on your ultimatum? But you were expecting that. She'll ask you back in a day or two."

"I never got a chance to give her an ultimatum. Getting rid of me was all her own idea."

"Oh, Rusty, I'm so sorry. But I'm sure she'll change her mind after a few days. You said yourself that she'd miss you if you went away."

"I was wrong. Leslie had other plans all along, as it turns out. She's leaving Austin for California, and she wants to put her condo on the market."

"Leslie's leaving town? Just like that?"

"Just like that. She's been angling for a better job in the Silicon Valley, and one finally came through. Geez, Sarah, her career is more important to her than me."

He sounded so miserable, Sarah felt sympathetic tears fill her eyes. "You want to come over and cry on my shoulder?"

"I'll be right there," he said, hanging up the telephone immediately.

When Rusty arrived fifteen minutes later, he had a duffel bag with him.

"What's that?" she asked.

"Clothes and stuff. Is it okay if I hang out here for a day or two? I've kinda been moving from friend to friend. I don't want to wear out my welcome in any one place. Don't worry, it won't be for long. I'll find a place to live sooner or later."

She gave him a big hug. "You know you can stay as long as you want to. The couch makes into a bed."

Monday morning, Sarah was late for work. Having a guest, especially one who shaved, in a one-bathroom apartment had slowed her down. As soon as she was settled at her desk, she dialed Jake's number. She wanted to make certain he planned to see Dr. Johnson, first thing.

"Good morning, Mrs. Bradshaw. Is Jake—Mr. Logan in?"

"No, and I'm worried. He's never been this late before. He's never been late at all, come to think of it. He's always here when I arrive."

"He didn't call in?"

"No. I tried calling him, but he has his machine on."

A cold chill went through her. Something was wrong. She never should have let Jake drive home alone. She should have gone with him, and made sure he called the doctor. "I'm going to his house to check on him. He caught a bad cold in San Antonio. It must have gotten worse."

Jake heard the doorbell ring, but he didn't feel like moving. Every time he moved he discovered another place that ached—and he already knew that his head throbbed, his stomach hurt and his throat was on fire. He kept his eyes squeezed shut and prayed whoever was at the door would leave him to die in peace.

"Oh, Jake!"

He opened one eye. "Hello, Sarah." He sounded like a frog. If he were lucky, maybe she'd kiss him and turn him into a prince. He sat up and held out his arms. "Give us a kiss." He grimaced, and held his head in his hands. "Head hurts."

She sat down next to him. "Shh. Not now. Lean back and close your eyes."

Sarah began massaging his temples. Her fingertips were gentle. Soothing. Jake relaxed and let himself drift into unconsciousness. The last thing he heard was Sarah's voice telling him she was calling the doctor.

The next time he was aware of anything, Dr. Johnson was poking and prodding him as Sarah hovered in the background.

"Open wide. Say 'ah.'" The doctor frowned. "Now put this under your tongue. Close." Jake bit down on a thermometer—fortunately one made of plastic, not glass—and held it in place until it beeped.

After he checked the temperature, Dr. Johnson absently shook the digital thermometer and told Sarah, "He has the flu—a particularly nasty strain, I'd say. He must stay in bed, and he will need someone to stay with him. Jake's going to get worse before he feels better and he's too weak to take care of himself. I can arrange for a nurse, but—"

Jake forced himself to protest. "No nurse," he croaked. "I want Sarah."

Dr. Johnson began packing up his little black bag. "Can you stay with him?"

"Me? I'm not a nurse."

"He doesn't need an R.N., just someone to feed him juice and aspirin. You can handle that."

"I don't know. For how long?"

"Three or four days. A week at the most."

Jake groaned. She wasn't leaping at the chance to take care of him. He couldn't blame her. She was probably remembering his nasty remarks yesterday. He should never have accused her of being more interested in his money than in him. He grabbed her hand and held on. "Please stay with me, Sarah. I need you."

"All right," she agreed, reluctantly it seemed to him. "You are the boss. But you'd better really be sick."

"He's really sick. No question about that." Dr. Johnson moved to the bedside table and pulled a pad from his pocket. He scribbled a few lines, then handed a piece of paper to Sarah. "Here's a prescription for an antibiotic. It won't help the flu, but we don't want it turning into pneumonia. Give him aspirin for the fever and keep him in bed. He's not going to want to eat much, but be sure he gets plenty of fluids. We don't want him getting dehydrated. I'll drop by tomorrow to check on him."

"I'll take good care of him, Dr. Johnson."

Jake let his eyes close and listened while Sarah moved around the room. He still ached all over, and he couldn't stop shivering, but he felt something warm and soothing spreading through his poor, battered body. Satisfaction. Sarah was going to move in with him.

He listened as she walked across the hall to his study and dialed the telephone.

"Hi. If you have time, I need a favor. I'm at my boss's house. He's got the flu, and I'm going to stay with him for a day or two."

Jake frowned. She was going to stay for a week. Hadn't she heard what Dr. Johnson said?

"Could you pack a bag for me?"

She must be talking to a girlfriend. Maybe Leslie Simmons. A satisfied smile curved his lips. Sarah wasn't going to leave him alone, not even to get what she needed.

"Great! I appreciate it. Jake lives on Lake Austin. Twenty-five twenty-three Camino Real. Thanks again."

A few minutes later, Sarah appeared at his side. She carried a glass of ice water and a bottle of aspirin. She handed him two tablets.

Tossing them into his mouth, he reached for the glass and washed them down with the cold water. It had a tangy flavor. "Lemon?"

"I squeezed a little in the glass. You can use the vitamin C. Wouldn't you be more comfortable in pajamas?"

Jake was wearing a sweat suit. "I don't have any pajamas. I sleep in the nude."

He finished the water. His hand shook slightly as he handed the glass to Sarah, but she didn't seem to notice. The last thing he wanted was for her to think of him as weak and helpless. She might pity him. Pity was not the emotion he craved from Sarah.

On that thought, he closed his eyes. When he opened them again he could tell time had passed from the shadows on the wall opposite his bed. He must have slept for an hour or two. Jake rubbed his eyes and glanced around the room. "Sarah?"

No one answered. Jake pushed back the covers and stood up. His legs wobbled, but he managed to make it to the top of the stairs, holding on to the wall.

"Sarah, where are you? I'm thirsty."

Jake heard her in the kitchen, opening cabinets. She turned on the faucet. He must be out of bottled water. He stumbled back to bed and waited.

Footsteps clumped up the stairs. Loudly. Sarah was usually very light-footed.

A large, red-haired man appeared in the doorway. He was holding a glass.

"Who are you? Where's Sarah?"

"She went to get your prescription filled. She asked me to stay with you until she got back. Here, I brought you some water."

There was a suitcase next to the door. Jake recognized it as the one Sarah had taken to San Antonio. "Did you bring that?" he asked.

"Yeah. Sarah asked me to."

Jake eyed the man balefully. He didn't like the idea of Sarah asking this guy to pack her clothes. That struck him as being an intimate kind of favor for a man to do for a woman. He took the glass and cautiously ventured a small taste.

"Tap water." He curled his lip. "It's not even cold. And Sarah always squeezes a lemon in it. She says I need vitamin C. What did you say your name was?"

"Rusty Hansen. Sorry about the water. I'll get you some ice if you want."

"Never mind." He set the glass on the table.

The redheaded giant watched him in silence for several minutes. "How do you feel?"

"Rotten."

"Sarah's going to stay with you for a day or two."

"Yes, she's going to take care of me." Jake smiled smugly.

Rusty leaned over him. He did not smile back. "Don't do anything to hurt her."

"Excuse me?" With an effort, Jake raised his head off the pillow and glared at Hansen. Who did this guy think he was, Sarah's guardian redneck?

"You don't look like you could hurt a fly, right now. But you could get better." Rusty sounded as if he did not approve of Jake getting well. "When that happens, remember one thing—Brannan women don't fool around."

Jake closed his eyes and let his head fall back into the pillows. "So I've heard."

"Yeah? Who—oh, I know. Vince and Colt."

"Right." Jake pushed the blankets off himself. "It's too hot in here. How about opening the window?"

"Not a good idea. A blue norther moved in last night and it's real cold out there. If you're hot, it damn well better be a fever that's making you that way."

"What else would it be?" Jake asked testily. He was getting a little tired of Rusty's not so subtle threats. If he felt better, he'd take great pleasure in matching him glare for glare.

"Could be the thought of Sarah spending the night that's heating you up."

Jake nodded and closed his eyes. "You're right, Hansen. That might do it."

A hand the size of a ham came down on his forehead. "Nope. It's not Sarah that's got you hot. You've got a fever. Where do you keep the aspirin?"

"I don't know. Sarah will find it. Why don't you go away? I need to rest."

"I'm going. But if you do anything, any little thing to upset Sarah, I'll be back."

Jake squirmed uncomfortably. What did this Rusty character think he was going to do to Sarah? Break her heart? "What's between me and Sarah is none of your business. But, since you seem to be concerned, I swear I have no intention of hurting her."

Rusty pinned him with another menacing look. Then he nodded. "I'll go downstairs to wait for Sarah, then."

A few minutes later, Jake heard the sound of voices in the foyer. The front door closed, and then Sarah was standing in the doorway. She'd come back. A breath he hadn't known he'd been holding wheezed from his lungs. He smiled at her.

"Rusty said you were thirsty. I bought some juices at the drugstore. Would you like apple, grape or orange?"

"Just water. With a little lemon in it."

"He also said you were feverish again." She plumped his pillows and felt his forehead. "You don't feel too warm right now. Dr. Johnson said the fever would probably be at its highest at night, but I'll get you another dose of aspirin."

When she returned with the water and the aspirin, she gave them to him, then looked around the room.

"What are you looking for?"

"Somewhere to sleep. You don't have a cot, or an air mattress, do you?"

"No."

"And only that chair in the study. I can't sleep sitting up. I've tried."

"What's wrong with the guest room?"

"It's on the first floor—too far away. I'm afraid I won't hear you."

"Hear me what?"

"If you call out in the night. You may need me."

"Oh, yeah. I will. I do. You better stay close to me."

"I know." She looked around the room again. "I guess I'll make a pallet and sleep on the floor. It won't be the first time."

He patted the bed. "What's wrong with this?"

"You're in it."

"Afraid you won't be able to keep your hands off me?"

"More like vice versa."

"How can you say that? I'm a sick man."

"Uh-huh."

"And this is a king-size bed. I don't want you to sleep on the floor."

"We'll talk about it later. Do you think you'll be all right if I leave you alone for a while? I need to check your pantry to see how we're fixed for food. I may have to go to the grocery store."

He didn't want her to go. It was worth having the flu to have her fuss over him. No one had ever taken care of him before. "I'm not very hungry," he said mournfully. "I don't want you to go."

"Then I won't leave. I'll just go unpack. I'll be back in a flash and I'll read to you."

He yawned. "That would be nice. And I think I'll want some grape juice, too."

Jake settled back against the fluffy pillow and let his eyes drift shut. Being sick wasn't half-bad, not with a nurse like Sarah.

Later that night when he was throwing up his socks, he reconsidered. Being sick was hell. And he didn't like Sarah seeing him clutching the toilet bowl, helpless and disgusting.

When he'd finished, she helped him stand and gave him a glass of water. "Rinse out your mouth and brush your teeth."

"Okay. Leave me alone for a few minutes, will you?" He swayed against the sink. "I need a shower."

"You can't take a shower. You can't even stand up."

"Can, too," he grumbled.

She tugged on his sweatshirt. "Back in bed, buster."

Jake felt his lower lip push out. He was pouting, just like a spoiled little kid. He couldn't seem to help himself. "I want a shower," he sniveled.

"I'll give you a hospital bath." She put her arm around his waist and urged him out of the bathroom. "I know how to do it. I took a course in home health care one summer to earn a Girl Scout badge. I can change the sheets, too—with you in the bed—and get you fresh pajamas."

"I told you—I don't have any pajamas."

"You do now. I borrowed a pair from a friend."

"You're going to give me a bath? Change my pajamas?" He collapsed onto the bed.

"I sure am." She pushed up the sleeves of her sweater and advanced on him.

"You're going to do all that when I'm in no condition to enjoy it?" Even though his stomach had settled, his head was swimming and he ached all over. And Sarah's hands were going to be all over him. He stifled a moan. "That's cruel, Sarah."

She laughed at him. "It is not. You're going to feel much better once you're all clean and tucked in for the night."

"Are you going to sleep with me?" He didn't know why she'd want to, now that she'd seen him with his head over the toilet bowl. On the other hand, if she hadn't fled in disgust after that, there was hope—

"Not a chance," she said repressively. "You're much too frisky. I'm beginning to think you don't have the flu at all. It could be a twenty-four-hour virus."

Jake flung one arm over his eyes and groaned. Sarah was by his side in an instant, feeling his forehead. "What's wrong? Is your stomach still upset? Should I call the doctor?"

"No, I'll be all right," he said, trying to convince himself he felt better. He wanted to be strong for Sarah, but he was as weak as a kitten. But even a sick kitten could enjoy being petted. "Just don't leave me."

"I'm not going anywhere. Not until you're completely well."

Keeping his arm over his eyes, he groped for her hand with his other hand. Once he felt her fingers close around his, he allowed himself to relax. "Can I have my bath now?" he asked, being sure to make the plea humble. It wouldn't do for Sarah to know how much he was looking forward to his bath.

She just might send him to shower alone.

Chapter Seven

Sarah eyed Jake nervously. The last time she'd given anyone a hospital bath, she'd been thirteen years old and the patient had been a store mannequin donated to her Scout troop by Bailey's Department Store. The mannequin had not been anatomically correct. Jake was.

Rubbing her damp palms on her slacks, she approached the bed. "Well, I guess we should get you nak—undressed before I get the hot water and soap." She pulled back the blankets and took Jake's sweatshirt by the hem. "Can you sit up?"

"Sure." Jake stayed flat on his back. "In a minute."

"Never mind." Gently, she pushed the sweatshirt up, her palms grazing sweat-dampened skin. When the shirt was bunched under his armpits, she told him, "Raise your arms."

Jake opened his eyes a slit. "Is this a holdup?" He closed his eyes, but he dutifully flopped his hands over his head. She pulled one sleeve free, covering his face in the process.

"I can't breathe!" Jake struggled weakly, managing to get his free arm back into the sleeve. His head was still buried in the folds of the bulky sweatshirt.

"Good grief! I bet Florence Nightingale never had to put up with this," Sarah sputtered, jerking the shirt over Jake's head in one swift movement.

Jake's head flopped back on the pillow. His eyes closed, he let out a moan.

"Oops. Sorry. Was I too rough?"

He opened his eyes and managed a feeble leer. "Like it rough. Hot, fast and rough. How's about you?"

Sarah felt her cheeks grow warm as Jake's words—slurred though they were—created disturbing images in her mind. "Jake Logan! Behave yourself, or I'll leave you the way you are."

His mouth drooped into a pout.

She pulled down the sheet and untied the cord on his sweatpants. Averting her eyes, she stripped off the pants, and without missing a beat, tossed the covers back on top of him. "Stay there while I get the water."

Sarah went to the bathroom and filled the large plastic dish pan she'd found earlier with warm water. Gathering towels from the linen closet, she tossed a washcloth and bar of soap into the pan and took everything to the bedroom.

She almost dropped the heavy pan of water when she saw what Jake had done. He'd kicked the covers almost all the way off.

"Jake! Don't do that. You'll get chilled."

"Hot," he muttered, kicking his feet free of the last blanket.

Sarah stared. A tiny voice, one that sounded a lot like Granny Brannan, told Sarah she should modestly avert her eyes. She ignored the voice, until Jake turned his head and caught her drooling over him.

"Like what you see?" he asked, his eyes drifting shut again.

Sarah jerked her gaze back to Jake's face. "Nothing I haven't seen before," she said, feigning a nonchalance she definitely didn't feel. She reflected that she was getting very good at lying. She'd never seen anything like Jake Logan before. Michelangelo's *David* came close—but cold marble could not compete with warm flesh.

Not so warm—Jake had goose bumps. This was not the time for lecherous thoughts. She had to get him washed, dried and dressed quickly—for his health and her virtue. Grabbing a washcloth and a bar of soap, she vigorously soaped the cloth, then took a swipe at Jake's chest.

He groaned loudly. Startled, she looked up at him. "What's wrong? Is the water too hot?"

His eyes opened a slit. "You're wearing clothes. You're not supposed to wear clothes in the shower."

"We're not in the shower. I'm giving you a bath." Telling herself it would all be over soon, Sarah continued soaping Jake's chest. Briskly. This was no time to linger over hard muscles and a hair-roughened chest. "Turn over and I'll wash your back."

He obeyed, but twisted his head around to look at her. "The sheets are wet," he mumbled. "Your sweater's getting wet, too. Don't you want to take it off?"

She eyed his over-the-shoulder innocent gaze. Was he flirting or delirious? Giving him the benefit of the doubt, she slid the washcloth across his shoulder and down his spine. Either way, she was pretty sure he was all talk and no action.

She had the washcloth at his waist now. Hesitating for only a second, she gingerly stroked the wet cloth across his buttocks. He shivered. She jumped. "That's enough," she said. She'd missed a few spots, but she couldn't touch him any longer—one person with a fever was all she could handle. It wouldn't do for her to go up in flames.

"You need to be warm and dry." Sarah grabbed a towel and rubbed his back. "I'll change the sheets now. Then I'll get you into some nice clean pj's."

"Thanks for the bath," he mumbled.

She glanced at him suspiciously. She wished she knew for sure that he was too sick to have enjoyed it. "You're welcome. I think."

Jake yawned. "Sleepy."

"Go to sleep then. You need rest."

"Sleep with me. I'll rest better if you're in bed with me."

"Good grief! Don't you ever turn it off?"

"Not when you've got your hands all over me. Or almost all over. Didn't you forget a few places?"

"None of the important ones."

Face flaming, Sarah finished drying him off, then changed the wet sheets. After she got him into the pajamas she'd borrowed from Rusty, she took his temperature. "Ninety-nine point six. Not normal, but not too bad," she muttered. "How do you feel?"

He didn't respond. His eyes were closed and his skin had an unnatural pallor, but his breathing appeared regular. She watched as his now decently covered chest rose and fell, remembering how it had looked wet and naked.

With a guilty start, Sarah put the thermometer away and went to get her suitcase from the study. She dressed for bed in an oversize Texas Longhorn football jersey. She'd brought along a black satin nightshirt, too, but that recent purchase would be wasted on Jake now. Not only that, tantalizing a man as sick as he was with sexy nighties was probably going too far, even for a Brannan woman. She was learning that not quite everything was fair in love and war.

She hurried back to Jake's bedside. Touching his forehead and finding it no warmer than when she'd left him, she got up and walked around to the empty side of the bed. It was a very large bed and she was very tired. Surely it wouldn't hurt if she rested her eyes for a moment before she looked for quilts and blankets to make a pallet on the floor. She lay down next to Jake.

Just before her head hit the pillow, she jerked upright. "No, no, no! Are you crazy, or what?"

Hastily getting out of Jake's bed, Sarah went to the linen closet in the bathroom. She needed a good talking to, and there was no one around to provide one, except her.

Grabbing sheets and blankets off the shelf, she muttered, "Jake already got you to spend the night—several nights—under his roof. You're practically living with him! Which is exactly what he wanted."

She stared into the mirror over the sink. "Are you going to let him have everything he wants? What would Barbara and Laura say?"

She sneered at her reflection. "I know exactly what they'd say. Large bed. Ha! You're tired. Double ha-ha! What you are, my girl, is hot and bothered and ready to do something about it. Once you were in bed with Jake, how long do you think you would have stayed on your side?"

Her reflection didn't answer. Just as well, since she knew exactly what would have happened if she'd tried to sleep in Jake's bed. She'd have been drawn to him like steel to a magnet. Only she wasn't cold, hard metal. She was warm flesh and blood, and she yearned to be close to the man she loved.

She folded one blanket in half and spread it on the floor next to his bed. "Here's where you belong, Sarah Jane Brannan. Alone on the cold, hard floor. If you can't control your urges, you're going to ruin everything."

Sarah went to sleep murmuring, "Jake needs a wife not a lover. Jake needs a wife not a lover."

She didn't stay asleep for long. Jake spent a restless night, alternating between delirium and a frightening stillness that she hoped was only a deep sleep. She managed to get more aspirin down him every few hours, making him drink as much water as he'd swallow.

Near dawn, just as she was about to drift off to sleep, Jake began thrashing about on the bed. He was talking, too, but the words were slurred and unintelligible. Sarah got up and looked at the clock. It was too soon for another dose of aspirin and antibiotics.

Sitting next to him on the bed, she began stroking his brow. "Shh. Jake, try to sleep. You need rest, darling. You'll feel much better after a good night's sleep." She yawned hugely. "So will I," she murmured, before continuing to soothe him with her words and her hands.

Jake finally stilled. Sarah started to get up and return to her bed on the floor, but the minute she took her hand from Jake's forehead, his eyes opened. The dawning day lightened the room enough that she could see his eyes were bright.

"I love you, Sarah," said Jake distinctly. "Will you marry me?"

Sarah fell off the edge of the bed. Sitting on the floor rubbing her tailbone, she gaped up at him. "What did you say?"

"I love you, Sarah," he repeated. "Marry me?" He was grinning at her, a boyish, vulnerable kind of grin. She tried to look into his eyes, to see if love or fever was shining there, but her own vision was blurred by tears.

"Oh, Jake! Of course I'll marry you. I love you, too." She moved to a kneeling position and put her arms around him. She gave him a fierce hug. "You've made me so happy. I'll be the best wife in the world, I promise."

She babbled on for minutes, before she realized Jake had fallen asleep again. Sarah returned to the pallet, but the floor seemed even harder now that she was wide-awake. Tossing aside the covers, she got up. After tucking Jake in one more time, dropping several kisses on his sleeping face in the process, she floated down the stairs.

She filled the teakettle with water and put it on the stove, then went to the telephone. It wasn't quite 6:00 a.m., but the Brannans were all early risers. She couldn't wait to tell them about her new status as an engaged woman.

"Good morning!" Sarah stood in the doorway, holding a large steaming mug in her hand.

Jake blinked at the brilliance of Sarah's smile. He'd always thought her smiles were worth working for, but she'd never smiled at him like this.

"Do you feel like eating something, darling, or do you just want tea? I put honey in it. Granny Brannan always made us hot tea with honey when we were sick. She said it was good for what ails you."

Darling? He must be dreaming. He had been dreaming, now that he thought about it. About wives and weddings and other unspeakable horrors. Jake shuddered.

Sarah was at his side in an instant. She put her hand on his forehead. "You're not warm. But you're shivering like you're having chills. I'd better take your temperature." She looked around. "What did I do with the thermometer?"

"I don't have a fever and I'm not cold. If I'm shaking it's because I was remembering a bad dream."

"Let's just make sure." She set the mug of tea on the bedside table and picked up the thermometer.

Popping it in his mouth, she asked, "Are you hungry?"

Shaking his head, Jake struggled into a sitting position. Talking around the thermometer, he said, "My stomach still feels kind of queasy."

"Just tea and juice for now, then." She removed the thermometer. "You were right. Normal." Taking the pillow from the bed, she fluffed it, then put it behind his back. Handing him the mug, she watched approvingly as he sipped the hot, sweet tea.

When he'd emptied the mug, she took it from his hand and put it on the table. She touched his face gently. "Do you want me to shave you?"

Jake rubbed his chin. His whiskers were stiff and bristly. "I must look like hell."

"You look sexy." Her voice was low and husky and she didn't bother to disguise the longing in her eyes.

Bemused, Jake leaned against the headboard. "Sexy? Me?" He couldn't keep a satisfied grin off his face. "You think so? It must be the whiskers. Maybe I'll forget about shaving for a day or two."

"Will you be all right by yourself for a few minutes? I need to go to the grocery store for more juice and for chicken soup ingredients." She straightened the sheet and duvet as she talked, smoothing the covers around him. "You do like chicken soup, don't you? It's good for you, and we've got to get you well as soon as possible. There's so much for us to do."

"I like chicken soup," he said. He liked Sarah's pampering even more. "What do we have to do?"

Sarah laughed. "Men. You are so oblivious. Don't worry about it. I'll take care of everything." She walked out the door, then stuck her head back around the doorframe. "Is there anything you need before I go?"

"A kiss goodbye."

Surprisingly, Sarah was at his side before he could blink. She touched her lips to his forehead, then kissed him full on the mouth. "Try to go back to sleep, sweetheart. You couldn't have gotten much rest last night."

She left again, only to return almost immediately. "I do need some input from you, after all. How do you feel about Christmas?"

He stared at her. "I'm in favor of it," he said, cautiously.

She giggled. "Me, too. I'll be right back, dear," she promised, flashing him another of those brilliant smiles.

Dear? Darling? She'd never used endearments like that before. And she'd kissed him without an argument. What was going on? Jake leaned back against the fluffed pillows and began to analyze Sarah's bewildering actions. He didn't get very far. Insufficient data was the last thought he had before drifting off to sleep.

When he woke, he could hear Sarah moving around in the kitchen, and a delicious odor was wafting up the stairwell, making his stomach growl.

While he'd slept, his subconscious had come up with an answer to explain Sarah's behavior. Sarah was softhearted, and seeing him weak and helpless from the flu must have engaged her tenderest feelings. Pity. She felt sorry for him.

Disgusted, Jake tossed aside the covers and moved his legs over the side of the bed. His pajama-clad legs.

Where had the pajamas come from? He pulled the pajama top away from his body and peered inside. There was a lot of room. Sarah could get in here with him. Jake smiled, thinking of him and Sarah trapped together in a pair of extra, extra large pj's.

Something clicked. He knew only one man that size. That redheaded giant who'd snarled at him about not hurting Sarah. These were his pajamas. Sarah must have borrowed them from Hansen.

Jake stood up and untied the cord at his waist. He wasn't going to wear another man's pajamas. He wasn't as needy as that.

He stripped them off. His bathrobe was draped on a pile of blankets and pillows on the chair next to his bed. He put it on and crossed the hall to his study.

It was a mess. Sarah must have been there. He walked over to the desk, which was littered with telephone books—white and yellow pages—and pieces of paper. Picking up one of the sheets, he discovered she had been writing out a list. That was a good sign. He believed in making lists. It was a simple way to set priorities. Plus, checking off each item as it was done was enormously satisfying.

Aspirin was at the top of the list, followed by juice, chicken, egg noodles—a grocery list. Leave it to Sarah to make a list and forget to take it with her. Judging from the tantalizing smells, she hadn't forgotten any of the chicken soup ingredients.

Grinning, Jake dropped the grocery list onto his desk and picked up another sheet of paper. Invitations, this one said. The list continued with flowers, cake and Reverend Martin. Sarah had doodled on the margins of the paper—two hearts entwined, with the initials SJB in one, JAL in the other. She'd written his name, too, several times. Jacob Allan Logan.

Jake looked closer and his heart began to pound ominously. Something was very wrong. His name had a "Mrs." in front of it.

Sarah was planning a wedding. Their wedding.

"Sarah!" he yelled, panic-stricken.

She came racing up the stairs. "Jake! Where are you? What's wrong?"

"In the study." Jake sat down heavily in the leather recliner as Sarah entered the room. She was carrying a magazine. A bridal magazine. He groaned.

"Why did you get up? You march yourself right back across that hall and get into bed. You're not well, Jake."

"What's this about, Sarah?" He waved the list at her.

"I made a list of everything we have to get done before Christmas. What's wrong with that? I thought you approved of lists."

"I do. You're planning our wedding, aren't you?"

"Well, yes." She put her hand over her mouth, her eyes wide. "Oh, Jake, I'm sorry. I should have waited until you were well enough for us to do it together. But I've waited so long, and I was so excited, I wanted to jump right in and get started. And we don't have much time, only three weeks or so, before Christmas. With so little time, it will have to be an informal wedding. Mom said we could be married at home, with only the family as guests. Barbara's going to make the wedding cake—she's very good at cake decorating. I didn't think you'd mind. But maybe you'd rather invite others and have a catered reception here in Austin. I wanted a Christmas wedding, but we could wait if you want a big, formal wedding. Valentine's Day would be nice, too. Maybe even better. Pink is my favorite color, and that would give us plenty of time to get invitations engraved and—"

Jake leaned over and hid his face in his hands. "I feel sick."

"Oh! How could I have been so thoughtless? Carrying on about wedding plans when you don't feel well." She knelt in front of him. "Jake, can you make it back to bed?"

He nodded. Opening his eyes, he let Sarah help him from the chair. Light-headed and disoriented, whether from the flu or Sarah's wedding fever he couldn't have said, Jake let her lead him back into his bedroom. Once he was tucked in again, she asked, "Are you hungry yet? The soup's ready."

He opened his mouth to tell her he wasn't going to marry her, but one look at her face made him nod in agreement instead. "I think I could eat a little something," he said carefully.

Time, he needed time to think about what to do. Time, and a clear head. His brain was short-circuiting, what with trying to cope with a virus and a misunderstanding of gargantuan proportions.

Where had Sarah ever gotten the idea that they were going to get married? He had been scrupulously honest with her from the beginning. He was never going to get married. Never. He had told her that, repeatedly. She knew how he felt about marriage. She'd even told him she had given up on trying to get him to the altar.

Maybe this was another Brannan woman trick.

If the victim didn't cooperate, she fabricated a proposal. It made a Sarah kind of sense—and it was devious and clever enough for a Renaissance prince. Had there been a Mrs. Machiavelli?

Jake shook his head. He had to admire the audacity that set such a diabolical snare, even as he squirmed in its coils. It put a man in the awkward position of either going along with the program, thereby ending up as a husband, or calling the woman a liar and ending up alone.

He wasn't going to give up. There had to be a way out of this trap. Now that he finally had Sarah in his house, almost in his bed, he wasn't about to wave the white flag of surrender. Not yet.

Concentrating on his vital signs, Jake decided he was feeling much better, physically. But he'd feign illness until he'd reasoned out a solution to his problem. That way he could avoid any more talks about caterers and wedding cakes. He shuddered again, just as Sarah came in the room carrying a tray.

"Poor darling. You still have a fever and chills, don't you?"

He let his mouth droop, and nodded.

"Do you still want something to eat?"

His stomach growled. "I think I could manage a few swallows," he said mournfully.

"You won't have to do a thing, sweetheart. I'll feed you."

"Good soup," he said, when she'd given him the last spoonful.

"Thank you. Would you like anything else?"

A big juicy steak and a pile of French fries, he thought. Soup and juice were not enough, not when a man needed fuel to fight his way free of the marriage snare. "No, I'm feeling tired again."

Sarah put the tray on the bedside table and reached for the aspirin bottle. "I'll just give you these," she said, shaking out two tablets. "Then I'll leave you alone. Sleep will do you good."

Two days later, Jake still hadn't come up with a plan and he was starving to death. Plus he wasn't sleeping well. Every time his subconscious took over, he dreamed of orange blossoms and white lace. And a radiant Sarah walking down the aisle toward him.

It scared the hell out of him.

There was no way out. He had to tell Sarah he knew he had not proposed, even if it broke her heart. He couldn't risk marrying her, not when he knew what would happen if he let himself surrender to her siren call. It would hurt her, something he'd sworn not to do. But not as much as it would hurt both of them later. If he ended things now, he'd get over it, and so would she. Sarah would find her Mr. Right—a man who wasn't terrified of love and marriage.

He was mulling over when to tell her, and how, when she came up the stairs.

"Here's your mail." She gave him a lingering kiss on the mouth.

He laid the letters on the bed next to him. The confrontation could wait a while longer, he decided, as he tugged her down on top of him. Sweet passion flared in her sea green eyes. Sarah wanted him. Jake closed his eyes, not wanting to see the innocent trust that also shone in her gaze. Not now, when she was so soft and yielding. He found her mouth and kissed her hungrily.

When he paused for breath, she gasped, "You must be feeling better."

"Much better." He pulled her shirt loose from her jeans and slid his hands underneath, reveling in the silky feel of her skin. Holding her close, he rolled over, pinning her beneath him. He kissed her again, and began slowly opening the buttons on her shirt. Pushing the garment aside, he trailed one finger from the pulse beating frantically in her throat to the lacy bra covering her breasts. When he brushed his hand over one firm, round globe and felt her nipple harden in response, a shudder went through him. He wanted more.

Jake crushed her mouth with his, and felt a primitive triumph when Sarah's arms closed around his neck, and she strained against him. She was on the verge of surrender.

Because she thought he was going to marry her.

With a groan, Jake tore his mouth from hers and rolled off of her.

"Sarah, we need to talk."

"Oh. Is that what we need to do?" She sounded breathless.

They lay side by side for a few minutes, then Sarah sat up and began buttoning her shirt. When she stood, the letters she'd brought him tumbled off the bed onto the floor. She picked them up and handed them to him.

"Aren't you going to open your mail?"

"Later. Sarah—"

"There's an invitation. Looks like a wedding invitation. From Massachusetts. Isn't that where your parents live?"

He picked up the stiff white envelope and glanced at the postmark. "My mother does. Father lives in California now."

Jake opened the envelope and took out the engraved invitation. A sardonic grin crossed his face. If he believed in omens... With a shrug, he tossed the invitation aside. "Sarah—"

"May I?" Sarah picked up the invitation and read it. "Anne Palmer and Lawrence Caldicott are getting married. Who are they?"

"Anne Logan Boatwright Palmer is my mother."

Sarah looked at the invitation again. "Your mother's getting married in February? Well, that shouldn't interfere with anything. She'll be able to come to our wedding. Will we go to hers?"

"No. About our wedding—"

"I know. We should postpone it long enough to plan a formal wedding. I forgot you're from the East, and Easterners are much more formal. I mean, if this is your mother's fourth wedding, and she's sending out engraved invitations... But Valentine's Day will be here before we know it, and I know Mom would prefer a church wedding. Barbara and Laura both were married in our church. The fourteenth of February will be just fine. I can wait," Sarah said bravely.

Before Jake could open his mouth, Sarah's face fell. "Unless you think Valentine's Day is too close to your mother's wedding. I wonder why someone would get married in February and not choose Valentine's Day, the most romantic day of—"

"Sarah! Stop! We're not getting married Christmas Day or Valentine's Day. You know damn well I did not propose."

Her eyes opened wide. "Of course you did."

He crossed his arms over his chest and looked at her sternly. "I did not."

"Jake! You did propose. And I accepted. I wouldn't make something like that up."

"Wouldn't you?" Self-righteous anger began to overcome his guilt feelings. How dare she cling to her phony proposal story? "I did not ask you to marry me. You sure as hell made that up."

"I have never lied to you. And don't swear at me!"

"Never? Come on, Sarah! You said you'd given up on me. You told me you realized I was not the marrying kind so you were going to husband hunt elsewhere. That was a lie."

"A tiny, white lie. All's fair—"

"Wrong. I was fair with you. I told you from the beginning that I had no intention of ever getting married. I meant it. And I did not propose."

"You did, too. Lying right there where you're lying now. Monday night, no, Tuesday morning. You said, clear as anything, 'I love you, Sarah. Will you marry me?' You said it twice, Jake. Two times. The first time I was so surprised, I fell off the bed. But the second time I said, 'yes,' and then—"

"What?"

She paused. "You fell asleep—very suddenly. But you were awake when you proposed—your eyes were open and you spoke clearly."

Jake could see the uncertainty in Sarah's eyes. "I must have been out of my head."

"Crazy? You think you'd have to be insane to ask me to marry you?"

"Not crazy. Delirious."

Sarah opened her mouth, then closed it. Taking a deep breath, she said slowly, "This is important, Jake. You truly don't remember asking me to marry you?"

"I don't remember." Jake knew suddenly that Sarah hadn't lied to him. It was that dream again. He had been dreaming about Sarah.

"And you don't love me?" Her voice was husky and her chin was trembling.

She was going to cry. Hell. He couldn't stand it if she cried. "It's better this way, Sarah. You'll find someone—"

"Please, Jake. If you don't love me, tell me so and I'll leave you alone. I'd never marry a man who didn't love me."

He had to say the words. "I don't love you."

Chapter Eight

"For the last time, you're going with me and that's that." Sarah took a silver-and-glass ornament from the box at her feet and hung it on the tree. Rusty hung another silver ball right next to hers. She moved it. "Pay attention, Hansen. Vary the colors, will you?"

Rusty shrugged his shoulders and reached for another ornament. He obviously didn't care what the tree looked like. Too bad. They were going to decorate it right, if she had to personally rearrange every ornament he put on the tree.

"Why won't you go? What else do you have to do Friday night?"

"Suffer."

She slanted a glance at him. He didn't look any happier now than he had before she'd made him go with her to buy the Christmas tree. Rusty hadn't wanted to acknowledge the season, but that hadn't stopped her. She'd bought a tree and lights and boxes of ornaments. Oh, he'd tried to get in the mood, she had to give him that. He had bought the tree-topper all by himself.

She could definitely empathize with Rusty's foul mood. She'd planned on spending the week before Christmas being miserable and lonely, crying her eyes out, but she'd changed her mind.

No man was going to ruin her Christmas. Or her life.

Rusty had offered his shoulder the day she'd come back from Jake's, heartbroken and mad as hell at the male sex. But one good cry was all Jake Logan was worth. And how could she be lonely when she tripped over the Incredible Redheaded Hulk every time she turned around?

She'd forced herself to cheer up. She wasn't exactly happy, but she'd definitely moved beyond sorrow to indignation. How dare Jake think she'd lied about his proposal? She reached for another glass ornament. Jake Logan was a jerk. And Jake the jerk had to pay for what he'd done.

Plotting revenge was definitely better than wallowing in self-pity. Sarah hummed a few bars of "Deck the Halls" as she hung the last red ball on the tree. "We're almost done. Then we can talk."

"I hate it when a woman says that. What's so important about talking? I bet you want me to get in touch with my feelings, right? Forget it. I've been in touch. I feel lousy. I don't want to talk about it."

"Neither do I. I want to talk about Christmas. Parties. Cheerful stuff. What's wrong with that?"

Rusty sighed. At least she assumed that mournful rumble was a sigh. She was beginning to get a tad disgusted with him. Here she was, acting like one of Santa's elves, as well as his gracious hostess, and he was resisting doing one tiny little thing for her.

Rusty had decided to stay at her place through the holidays, while he searched for a new apartment. If she'd been inclined to be uncharitable, she might have suspected him of hanging around for the sole reason of keeping her company—as in misery loves company. She refused to be miserable. She wasn't going to let Rusty be that way, either.

"I'm not going to the Loganetics Christmas party," he muttered, draping a single tinsel icicle on a branch above her head.

"Double-dog dare you," she drawled, watching him out of the corner of her eye.

He stiffened in reaction to the old childhood taunt. "I don't do dares anymore. You don't need me. You can go partying all by yourself." He hung another icicle on the tree.

"Are you going to put those on the tree one at a time?"

"Yes."

"We'll never finish if you do it that way." She grabbed the package, took out a handful of tinsel and threw it at the tree. "There. Now we're done. Except for the angel. You did get an angel, didn't you?"

"Yes, I got the angel. It's in that box on the coffee table." He took a step back and looked at the tree. "If you had to get a tree, why didn't you get a little one? Why did you buy this seven-foot-tall monster?"

"It was the only one left that had any shape to it. Lighten up, Mr. Scrooge. Get in the Christmas spirit. Let me hear a few fa-la-las."

"I don't see why you're so happy. I thought your heart was broken, too."

"I'm faking it—laughing through my tears, so to speak. You ought to try it. After a while, you'll forget you're fooling yourself. You might even start to feel like going to a Christmas party."

He shook his head vigorously. "Not a chance. You can go without me."

"No, I can't. I am not going alone. I will not let that man see me at the party all by myself."

"Tough. I don't want to see Leslie with another man."

"Why not? She didn't leave you for another man."

"Thanks for reminding me. Being dumped for a career opportunity is so much easier on the ego."

"You don't have to get sarcastic. Why she dumped—left you—isn't important. The woman is seriously flawed. She wasn't worthy of you."

"That's not what you said when you introduced us. Face it, Brannan. I don't owe you a thing. You owe me."

"Trust you to throw that in my face. I never claimed to be any good at matchmaking. And exactly what do I owe you?"

"Peace and quiet. I want to be left alone." He frowned and tilted his head to one side. "Are you sure this tree is straight? I think it's listing to the left."

"Forget the tree. You need to go to the Christmas party. You need to see Leslie one last time."

"No, I don't. I remember everything about her. I'm trying to forget." He frowned. "I don't understand why you're so hot to go to the damn party, anyway."

Sarah winced when she thought about the last time Jake had seen her. After he'd told her he didn't love her, she'd turned on her heel and left. Without a word. Without a tear. That absolutely could not be Jake's last memory of a Brannan woman. She was going out with a bang, not a whimper. Jake Logan might have won the war, but he was going to know he'd been in a battle. "I want to go to the party. I have to see Jake one more time."

Rusty's eyes clouded. "I didn't see Leslie at all. She told me she was moving to California over the phone."

"I knew it! You have to see her one last time, too. You need closure."

"Closure? That's a woman's magazine word if I ever heard one. What in the hell is closure? Some chick thing?"

"No. Closure is something all you modern, sensitive males should know about."

"Well, what is it?"

"I don't have time to explain. But you need it, and you're going to get it. At the Loganetics Christmas party."

"What's really going on here? You're still after that Logan guy, aren't you?"

Her mouth dropped open. "I am not. I just want to have the last word, that's all."

"That's not all. I should have figured this out sooner. A Brannan woman never gives up on her man."

"I gave up on you, remember?"

"I was never the man for you. And you know it."

"What about our agreement? You're not backing out of our pact, are you? Just when it looks like we're both doomed to fall in love with the wrong people?"

"Stop avoiding the subject. Why do you really want to go to the Christmas party?"

"I told you. I want Jake to see me one more time—so he'll remember what he lost."

"Hasn't he seen you at work?"

"Jake hasn't been back to the office yet."

"He will be, eventually. Wait until then."

"I don't want to wait. The only reason I went back to work was to finish the TimeMaster manual and I'm almost done. Besides, seeing him at work wouldn't be the same. You wouldn't be there." Sarah batted her eyes at him.

"Don't flirt with me, you hussy. I know you're just practicing. You're going to do something really mean to that poor man, aren't you?"

"I am not. In the first place, Jake is not a 'poor' man in any sense of the word. He does not need or deserve your sympathy. I am not going to do anything to him, because in the second place, even a Brannan woman knows when the game is over. Jake Logan told me flat out—he doesn't love me."

"He said he loved you when he proposed," Rusty reminded her.

"He was asleep at the time."

"I never heard of a man lying in his sleep. I guess it's possible—"

"What did you say?" She'd heard him, but she wanted to hear it again. No one lied in their sleep.

Sarah smiled up at Rusty. Such a brilliant observation! Why hadn't she thought of that?

"I'll admit that some scummy members of my sex have been known to say those three little words to get what they wanted—but why would a man say he loved a woman to get what he didn't want? Married, that is."

Her heart was doing strange little flip-flops in her chest, but she couldn't get too excited. Not yet. But it was all she could do not to jump up and down—hope had her soaring skyward like a helium-filled balloon.

"Jake said he was having a bad dream," she pointed out, trying to slow down her wildly rebounding fantasy of a future with Jake. "The man dreams about marrying me and he wakes up screaming. You want to compare bruised egos?"

"Not today. Here, take this." He handed her a plastic angel complete with blond wig and blue glass eyes. And a very unangelic bosom.

"Where did you find this? She looks like Dolly Parton with wings. Trust you to find the tackiest angel in town."

Rusty ignored her, put his hands on her waist and lifted her up. "Put her on the treetop."

She did as she was told.

Rusty set her down and plugged in the lights. "There. All done."

Sarah looked at the lights twinkling merrily, and took a deep breath. The sweet smell of Christmas filled her nostrils. She had been right to insist on a tree. She didn't feel vengeful anymore—and the angel didn't look so tacky now that she was settled on the top of the tree.

Maybe Rusty was right about Jake, too. But she had to face it, she wanted him to be right. If he was wrong... "Are you sure men don't lie in their sleep?"

"I'm positive. Remember biology class—the section on the brain? What's in control when we dream?"

"The subconscious."

"Well? Don't you see? Subconsciously, he loves you. Something's making him suppress it."

Sarah's hope-filled balloon fell to the ground with a thud. She squirmed guiltily. "No, you're the one who doesn't see. I didn't tell you everything. If those words were lurking in Jake's subconscious, it has to be because I sent him a telepathic message."

"Telepathic message? What kind of nonsense are you spouting? You can't send messages by brain waves."

"I really didn't think I could. But maybe I did."

He sat down on the couch. Patting the seat next to him, he said, "Come here and tell me everything."

Sarah sat down. "I sat across the table from him and I concentrated very hard on the message."

"Which was?"

"'I love you, Sarah. Will you marry me?' Which just happen to be the exact same words he said to me."

"Wait a minute—across what table? I thought he was sick in bed."

"I didn't do it while he was sick. Using telepathy on a sick man is probably unethical or something. I'm talking about the night I thought he was going to propose—before Thanksgiving."

"That was weeks ago."

"So? There could be some sort of posttelepathic suggestion syndrome at work here. Maybe I just planted the seed that night, and it took this long to surface.''

''Delayed reaction telepathy? I don't think so, Brannan. If the man told you he loved you when he was sound asleep, believe it. What's not to love?'' He reached over and ruffled her hair.

Sarah pushed his hand away. ''But when he was conscious Jake said he didn't love me. And he denied even asking me to marry him.''

''That proves it—it's marriage that turns him off, not you. He's running scared, that's all. And if you don't chase him, he's liable to run straight into another woman's arms.''

''I said I'd leave him alone. I promised.''

''You weren't going to keep that promise, and you know it. You've been plotting against him for hours. Why else would you want to go to the party?''

''Okay, you're right. I wasn't going to keep that particular promise, but I didn't cross my heart and hope to die,'' Sarah said, defending herself. And if she'd been willing to break the promise for revenge, she sure wasn't going to balk at breaking it to find out if Jake really did love her. She wasn't about to let one little old promise stand in the way of their happiness. ''You have to take me to the party now, don't you see?''

Rusty shook his head. ''I don't know. If I do, you're going to owe me big time. And someday, I'll collect.''

''Oh, Rusty. Please, please take me. I swear you won't be sorry. You're going to feel much better after you tell Leslie goodbye face-to-face.''

''Uh-huh.''

"It won't hurt for Leslie to see you with another woman, either. Wait till you see me in my new dress." Sarah pictured the red Lycra-and-velvet dress Barbara and Laura had forced her to hand over her hard-earned money for. It was slinky and sexy and just the thing to give a man second thoughts.

"All right. I'll do it. I'll take you to the Christmas party."

She could have sworn the angel winked at her.

"Where do you keep this, Mr. Logan?"

Gail Maroney, one of the maids employed by the condominium association, held up something silky and black.

"I don't know. It's not mine. Throw it away."

Before she could respond, Jake snatched the garment out of her hand. "Never mind. I'll take care of it." The shiny material was cool to the touch, but holding it was burning his fingers. He held it up. "What is this thing, anyway?"

"It looks like a nightshirt. A woman's nightshirt."

"Women sleep in this kind of thing?"

Mrs. Maroney, who was fifty if she was a day, surprised him with a girlish giggle. "Eventually." She smirked at him.

He handed her the shirt. "Do something with it. I don't care what. I'm going to work."

On the drive to the office, Jake tried to make a mental list of the things he'd need to catch up on once he was behind his desk. Instead he found himself ticking off the mementos Sarah had left behind when she'd walked out of his house.

Item. One lacy pink bra, in the dirty clothes hamper, tangled with his smelly sweatshirt. The bra had smelled like the lavender scent Sarah always wore.

Item. A neatly folded pair of bikini panties—also pink—sandwiched between two pairs of his Jockey shorts in his underwear drawer.

Item. One black satin nightshirt, tucked between the cushions of his sofa.

Who knew what other booby traps lurked in his closet, in his sock drawer, in his study? He'd move. He'd just pack up and move.

No, he wouldn't bother to pack. He'd leave everything behind and start over.

No. He wasn't going anywhere. No trained-from-birth female trickster was going to chase him out of town.

Jake arrived at the office in a foul mood. He growled good-morning to the receptionist, then pushed open the door to his office suite so hard it banged against the wall.

Mrs. Bradshaw looked up, startled, as he stalked past her. "I didn't know you were coming in today. You look pale. Are you sure you're well enough to be at work?"

"I could run a marathon," he snapped. In record time, if a certain Brannan woman was on his tail. "Where's the mail?"

Mrs. Bradshaw, who'd once confessed she'd spent hours as a child with a broom handle up her back, straightened her spine even more. In a chilled voice, she told him, "On your desk, where it is every morning."

With a curt nod, he went into his office. Closing the door behind him, he walked over to his desk. A pile of mail, neatly stacked, waited for him. He sat down and went through it quickly, then again, more slowly.

"Mrs. Bradshaw!" he yelled, forgoing the office intercom.

She appeared in his doorway. "What is it?"

"Is this all there is?" He waved his hand over the letters and reports now scattered haphazardly over his desk.

"Yes, sir."

Mrs. Bradshaw never called him "sir." He must have really ticked her off. Taking a deep breath, Jake forced the snarl out of his voice. "Interoffice mail, too?"

"Every bit of it. Except emergency items David handled." David Young was Loganetic's executive vice president.

"What emergencies?"

"A delayed shipment to Dallas—turned out it was temporarily lost in transit by the carrier. They blamed it on the Christmas rush."

"Any personnel emergencies?"

"Not that I know of."

"No resignations?"

"One."

"Aha! I knew it. So she quit, did she?"

"Yes, she did. But I thought you knew about Leslie Simmons's resignation. She turned it in before you got sick."

"I knew about her. No one else?"

She shook her head.

He shoved a hand through his hair. "No one absent without leave?"

"No. Will that be all, sir?"

"Yes. No. Have you seen Miss Brannan today? I didn't notice her car in the parking lot."

"As a matter of fact, she arrived the same time I did this morning. Someone dropped her off. Sarah told me her car is in the shop."

Sarah hadn't quit her job. Muscles he hadn't known were tensed relaxed. "Thank you. That will be all for now." As she turned to go, he said, "I'm sorry for the way I grilled you."

Mrs. Bradshaw gave him a wary smile. "That's all right. I know you've been ill. You've gotten some color back now. Are you feeling better?"

"Much better, thank you."

"Will you be attending the Christmas party tomorrow night? I wouldn't ask, but the entertainment committee has a little something planned that requires your presence. Of course, if you're not up to it, they'll understand."

"The party is this Friday? I seem to have lost track of time."

"Tomorrow is the last Friday before Christmas."

"I'll be there." Alone. He briefly flirted with the idea of calling someone to go with him. His little black book was around here somewhere, and short notice or not, he knew several of the women listed there would jump at another chance with him. He reached for the telephone, then let his hand fall to the table. It wouldn't do any good to ask another woman out.

He didn't want any woman but Sarah Brannan.

And he'd almost had her! She'd been right there in his house. Sleeping in his bedroom, if not his bed. If only she didn't have that hang-up about marriage—

There was a way to get her where he wanted her.

He just had to say the words. How hard could that be? He didn't have any trouble saying "I love you" in his dreams. It was worth a shot—Sarah might settle for the words. He didn't even have to mean them. She would never question his sincerity, and besides, it wasn't a total lie. He cared about her more than he'd ever cared about anyone.

Hell, maybe what he was feeling was love. He had to admit he was sorely lacking in experience with that particular emotion. No one had ever loved him, before Sarah. He hadn't loved anyone since he was eight years old. Maybe it was time to try again.

But he could only risk so much. No matter how much he wanted Sarah, some consequences were too awful to bear. She would have to settle for what he could give her.

And that did not include a wedding ring.

But he could explain exactly why he couldn't marry her. He should have told her when the wedding invitation came from his mother—the fourth such invitation he'd received since his parents' divorce. His mother would be trying again with her fourth husband. His father was still with his second wife, as far as he knew. His parents—his mother, especially—were very good at loving and leaving.

Once he told Sarah about his family, if you could call it that, she'd have to see why he couldn't take a chance on marriage. Marriage wouldn't last.

And what if they had children before they divorced? Sarah wanted children, he was sure of that. Something deep inside of him stirred as he thought of Sarah round and blooming, carrying his child. He pushed the thought away. That was a vision better left unseen.

He'd lost what family he had at the age of eight, and he'd always known he'd never have another one, even the temporary kind his mother favored. Not that Sarah would ever send a child of theirs away to boarding school when they divorced. He sure as hell wouldn't. Even so, a child deserved Sarah's kind of family—and that meant both parents, together, forever.

For him, the concept of forever did not compute.

Chapter Nine

"Do you see him?" Sarah stood behind Rusty. His broad shoulders made a convenient place to hide behind while she tried to calm down. Her palms were sweaty and those pesky butterflies were back.

She poked Rusty in the back. "Well? Do you? Is he with anyone?" She hadn't even thought about what she'd do if Jake had a date for the Christmas party—not until they'd entered the ballroom of the hotel where the festivities were occurring.

"No. I don't see Leslie either, thank God. Geez, Sarah! How many people work for Loganetics, anyway?"

"Several hundred." And most of them must have arrived promptly at eight—the time specified on the invitation. She and Rusty were late. She'd dithered.

Rusty reached behind him and grabbed Sarah's hand. "Come on. Let's mingle."

Taking a deep breath, Sarah followed in Rusty's wake. "Not so fast, Hansen. I'm not used to these three-inch heels." She looked at her red satin sandals. "Maybe this wasn't such a good idea."

"The shoes?"

"No, chasing after Jake."

"It was your idea, and you're stuck with it." Rusty dragged her into the mob of celebrants, then came to a sudden stop. "There he is."

Sarah stood on tip toe. "Where?"

"By the buffet table."

The crush of people made it impossible for her to see. Rusty, towering above her and ninety-nine percent of the other people present, did not have that problem. "Is he alone?"

"Hard to tell. There are women around him, but other men, too."

The butterflies were doing a polka. She might as well join them. "Let's dance."

"Dance? Don't you want to get something to eat first?"

"Are you crazy? We didn't come here for food." She didn't want to be anywhere near the buffet table and Jake Logan, not until she could project an aura of poised sophistication. Polite indifference, would work, too, at least until she thought of a way to get Jake to tell her he loved her. When he was awake.

"Well, let's find Logan, then."

"I'm not ready. Dance with me, Rusty."

"Chicken," he taunted.

"Turkey."

Rusty groaned. "Stop that. I'm hungry." But he took her in his arms and twirled her away from him, then drew her back. They always had danced well together—not surprising, since Rusty was the one who'd taught her how.

"I see Leslie," Sarah said. "No, don't turn around, just dance backward for a few steps."

"Girls dance backward," Rusty muttered, but he did as he was told. A few steps and they collided with Leslie and her partner. "Oops. Sorry about that."

"Rusty. Sarah. Merry Christmas." Leslie was calm and collected. Running into an old flame didn't appear to bother her in the slightest. Of course, she was the dumper, not the dumpee. That had to make a difference, confidence-wise.

"What's merry about it?" Rusty growled.

"Let's change partners," said Sarah brightly. "You two probably have things to talk about." Taking Leslie's partner by the hand, Sarah pulled him away.

After a moment's hesitation, Rusty took Leslie in his arms and they two-stepped into the crowd.

Sarah looked at the bewildered man left standing next to her. "Dance?" she asked, feeling conspicuous standing still in the middle of the dance floor.

"Oh, yeah. Sure." Once they were moving, he added, "I'm Oscar Raines."

"Sarah Brannan. Do you work for Loganetics?"

"Not yet. But I start next week, after the New Year. As a programmer. Leslie was on the interview team that hired me. That's how we met. Do you work there?"

"For now. But I'll be leaving soon."

"Really? Leslie's leaving, too. Is there a lot of turnover at Loganetics?" He sounded worried.

"Hardly any. It's a great place to work." As long as you don't fall in love with the boss, she reminded herself. Sarah looked over Oscar's shoulder, trying to catch a glimpse of Jake. The music stopped before she'd located him.

Sarah managed a friendly smile for her partner. "Well, I hope you enjoy your new job." She left Oscar at the edge of the dance floor and searched the room for Rusty. She saw his red head disappearing through the door to the ballroom. Leslie was with him.

She started after them, then halted. Rusty needed some time alone with Leslie. But without him to guard her, she felt like a quarterback out of the pocket—much too vulnerable. She began a casual stroll around the perimeter of the ballroom. Tables ringed the dance floor, and it appeared many of the guests were dining.

Sarah walked slowly, keeping in the shadows as much as possible as she searched for Jake. When she found him, what would she say to him? What would he say to her?

What if he didn't talk to her at all?

Long before she'd come up with a plan, Sarah spotted Jake. He was seated at a table with Mrs. Bradshaw and her husband. David Young and his wife, Mary, were at the table, too. No one else. It looked as if Jake had come to the party alone. Breathing a sigh of relief, Sarah backtracked and got in line for the buffet. Maybe eating a little something would soothe the herd of butterflies still frolicking in her tummy. She needed to be in full control of her senses when she confronted Jake.

When her plate was full, Sarah took it and sat down at a table on the same side of the room as Jake's, but slightly behind his. She could watch him, but unless he turned around, he wouldn't see her. Leaving the food untouched, she sipped a glass of champagne and gazed hungrily at Jake's profile. He looked so handsome in his tuxedo. Just as he might look waiting for her at the altar on their wedding day.

"And there will be a wedding day," she murmured. "We belong together, Mr. Logan, and tonight's the night you're finally going to admit that."

But how was she going to get him alone? What hould she do? Ask him to dance? Walk slowly by his able and see how he reacted to the red dress she was oured into?

She looked around the room again, as if the answer o her dilemma might be hiding somewhere in the reen garlands festooned with red ribbons. No soluions there, but Rusty was headed her way. He did not ook happy.

He sat down next to her. "Are you going to eat hat?"

"No. I couldn't eat a bite. Help yourself. How did go?"

Rusty ignored her and pulled the plate in front of im and shoved a piece of turkey in his mouth. He gnaled a waiter bearing a tray of champagne-filled lasses. When the waiter appeared, he said, "Leave the ay."

"Rusty! You can't drink all that."

"Watch me." He gulped down two glasses, then ached for a third.

She grabbed his hand and stood up. "Dance with me."

Rusty tugged on his hand, then looked her in the eyes. His own eyes were bleak. "I don't feel like dancing."

"Too bad. You didn't feel like decorating a Christmas tree, but you did it for me. Do this for me, too." She pulled him out of the chair.

Rusty took her in his arms. Sarah hugged him close. "It'll get better."

"I know." He gave a huge sigh, then rested his chin on the top of her head. "How are you doing? Did you see Logan?"

"Yes. He's at that table over there." Sarah indicated the location with a nod of her head. "Dance me that way."

"Your wish is my command. We'll show him what he let get away." Rusty began steering her in Jake's direction.

"Look. There's a mistletoe ball right in front of Jake's table. Do you think you could—"

"Leave it to me." Rusty maneuvered them to a spot directly in front of Jake's table. Tilting up her chin, he whispered, "Mission accomplished."

She turned her gaze up. They were directly under the mistletoe ball. "Well, what are you waiting for?" Standing on tiptoe, Sarah slid her arms around Rusty's neck. Rusty pulled her tight against him and lowered his head. Warm, familiar lips touched hers. Rusty Hansen had always been a good kisser. But his kisses had never affected her like Jake's. Maybe if she tried a little harder—

Sarah wound her arms around his neck and parted her lips.

Rusty pulled his head up. "Whoa, sweetheart. I think we got his attention," he said under his breath.

Someone tapped her on the shoulder. She turned her head and met Jake's gold-brown eyes. They were blazing like molten topaz. "May I have this dance?" he asked through clenched teeth.

Sarah's heart beat faster. "The music has stopped," she pointed out, her voice only a little bit shaky. "I think the band's taking a break."

"Fine, we'll sit this one out." He took her by one arm.

Rusty still had hold of her other arm. "Not with you, she won't. Sarah is my date." He pulled her toward him.

"She's my...employee." Jake jerked her toward him.

"This is a social occasion." Rusty pulled her back.

"It's an office occasion." Jake tugged.

"Office *party.*" Rusty countered, hauling her his way.

"Wait a darn minute!" Sarah yelled. "I am not a wishbone! Let me go, both of you!"

Both men released her simultaneously. She'd been leaning in Jake's direction to counter Rusty's pull, and when she lost her support, she tumbled against him. Jake's arms closed around her just as the music started up again. "My dance, I believe," he said coolly, whirling her away from Rusty.

He danced her out of the ballroom onto a deserted terrace. Late December was not the time to be out-of-doors, even in Texas. Jake, in a wool tuxedo, and mad as a hornet as far as she could tell, wasn't feeling the cold, but she was. Her strapless, backless dress was not designed for warmth. "It's a little c-chilly out here, don't you think?"

Jake pushed her farther away from the French doors that led to the ballroom, not stopping until her back was to the terrace balustrade. "What are you doing here?" he growled. "You said you weren't going to bother me anymore."

Her chin came up. "I d-didn't ask you to d-dance."

"No, you just planted yourself in front of me in that...dress and made a spectacle of yourself." Jake stripped off his jacket and wrapped it around her. "I should have known you'd never keep your promise. No woman who lies and cheats would balk at breaking a promise." His words were nasty, but his tone was resigned.

Sarah sucked in her breath. "I don't cheat!"

"You sure as hell don't play fair." He raised an eyebrow. "I notice you didn't deny lying."

"I—I may have fibbed a time or two. But only for your own good. According to Granny Brannan lies—little, white lies—are kinder than the truth sometimes."

"You lied to me for my own good?" He sounded incredulous.

"Yes. I did. You don't really want to be alone. I'm not the only one who thinks so. Barbara and Laura agree. And there's no reason for you to be paranoid about marriage. You did propose, you know, even if you were asleep when you did it. You said you love me, too. And you do. I know you do, no matter what you said later. Rusty says—"

He moved closer, so close they were almost touching, close enough to singe her with his angry, burning gaze. "Rusty. He keeps turning up. Why is that, Sarah?" Jake's voice was menacing.

"He's a friend. A very old, very dear friend. As a matter of fact, he's living with me—"

Jake grabbed her shoulders. "He's what?"

"Not living with me like you wanted me to live with you. His girlfriend kicked him out—that's a lesson for you, Mr. Logan. Living together doesn't work. It didn't for Rusty, and it wouldn't for me. Anyway, Rusty needed a place to stay for a few days. He needed cheering up, too, so I brought him to the party."

The fire in his eyes died down to a warm glow. "Did you need cheering up, too? Were you sad?"

She nodded, her face solemn. "Very sad. And lonely. I missed you."

The glow flared into golden flames. "So. Rusty is just a friend, and you missed me. If you're telling the truth, it follows that you must have kissed him for only one reason. To torment me." He bent his head until they were nose to nose. "Admit it."

"Were you tormented?" Sarah asked, clutching the lapels of his jacket and trying hard not to smile. She was almost sure he was teasing now, but caution seemed a wise course to follow until she was sure he was no longer angry.

"Damn right, I was. Get this straight, Sarah. You are not to kiss anyone but me."

Before she could blink, Jake swept her into his arms, crushed her against his chest and tilted up her chin.

"But Jake, I don't understand," Sarah protested. "You said you didn't love me. You accused me of tricking you into marriage. If you don't love me, then why—"

"Shut up and kiss me."

She looked up and saw nothing but stars. "There's no mistle— "

He groaned. "You talk too much." Jake's mouth covered hers. The minute his lips touched hers, she forgot about the cold. Kissing Jake was better than a roaring fire for getting warm. She let go of his coat and slid her arms around his neck. As he deepened the kiss, Sarah responded to the hunger she'd always sensed in Jake's kisses. That compelling need was what had been missing from Rusty's kiss, what made her want to give Jake whatever he longed for so desperately.

When he released her lips, she rested her forehead beneath his chin and sighed into his shirtfront. "Oh, Jake, I love you so much it hurts."

He stiffened, then relaxed. "I think I may love you, too."

Wide-eyed, she stared at him. "Oh, my goodness. There is a Santa Claus. Are you sure?"

"No. I am not sure. But I can't eat. I can't sleep without having night—dreams about you. You make my stomach hurt and my heart beat faster whenever you're near. I thought I was getting ulcers or having a heart attack the first few times that happened. I see you kissing another man and I want—simultaneously—to strangle you and kiss you senseless. Is that love?"

She tilted her head to one side, smiling tremulously. "I'm pretty sure." She felt his forehead. "But it might be another bout of the flu. Maybe you got out of bed too soon."

"I'm not sick. But I wouldn't mind getting back in bed. With you. Let me take you home."

"Rusty—"

"Is doing all right." He touched her cheek and gently turned her head toward the ballroom.

Through the French doors, she could see that Rusty was back at their table with another plate of food and a bottle of champagne. Several women had joined him.

"He always did have to beat them off with a stick." She gave Jake a tremulous smile. "All right. Take me home."

When they arrived at Sarah's, Christmas tree lights shone merrily through her front window. She gave him her key and he opened the door. Not bothering to turn on the lights, he closed the door behind them and took Sarah in his arms. She fit perfectly, her soft body molding willingly to his. The soft glow from the Christmas tree lights was reflected in her eyes, but something else shone brighter there. Love.

Sarah loved him. She'd give herself to him tonight. He was rock-solid certain of that. But first, he had to tell her—

He pulled her arms from around his neck. "Sarah, we have to talk."

She eyed him warily. "No, we don't. Trust me, Jake, the last thing we have to do tonight is talk. Didn't you just tell me I talk too much?"

"This is important."

"To quote a very smart man I know, shut up and kiss me." She slid her hands up his chest and untied his bow tie, all the while trailing kisses along his throat and jaw.

"Sarah—"

"Kiss me, Jake."

He couldn't resist her sweet demand. With a groan, he complied. Her mouth was soft and hot and he drank from it greedily. To his delight, Sarah responded immediately. As her lips parted, Jake pulled her closer and deepened the kiss. His whole body reacted instantaneously to the promises he tasted on her sweet lips. He could feel her heart pounding with a rhythm of desire echoed in his own blood.

With a rush of passion he could barely restrain, Jake fought for self-control. No matter how insatiably hungry he was for Sarah, he couldn't rush her. This was her first time, and he wanted to make it perfect for her.

He had to go slowly, handle her with all the tenderness he could muster. It wasn't going to be easy. He'd never felt like this before. With a groan, he ended the kiss. He had to stop, while he could still think. Reluctantly, he pulled his head up.

"Sarah, listen to me. If I love you—"

She put her hand over his mouth and gave him a severe look. "Nothing iffy about it. You love me, all right." She replaced her hand with her lips, kissing him on the mouth and then dropping small kisses on his jaw and throat.

"That doesn't change the fact that I can't marry you."

She stopped kissing him. "What? I don't understand."

"Turn on the lights, and I'll explain."

Sarah switched on the overhead lamp and sat down on the sofa. "This sounds serious. It's not just normal bachelor aversion to weddings, is it? It's more than that. Do you have some hereditary disease? Is that what's wrong? You don't want to pass the defective gene onto your children. That doesn't matter. We can adopt. Unless you don't want children at all?" She paused briefly to take a deep breath. "Well, that's okay, too. I can live with that. After all, I have lots of nieces and nephews. More on the way, probably—"

Jake sat down next to her and put his finger on her lips. "Hush, Sarah. I wouldn't call my problem a disease, but it's definitely hereditary." He leaned back and took a deep breath. "You know that my parents divorced when I was eight."

She nodded. "And they sent you to boarding school."

"It wasn't so bad—better than being at home in some ways. At least the teachers were trained to deal with children, unlike the maids and cooks who'd taken care of me up to that point. And there were other boys. I made a few friends."

"Oh, Jake!" Unshed tears shimmered in her emerald eyes. "How could they send you away?"

"Easy. They never wanted me in the first place. You have to understand about my father and mother. They both came from wealthy families, and all they really had in common was a desire to spend money as fast and frivolously as they could."

Sarah's love and compassion were washing over him in waves. He wanted nothing more than to take her in his arms and make sweet love to her, but he couldn't allow himself to do that, not until she faced up to the fact that he could never marry her. He got up and began pacing in front of the sofa.

"I didn't see much of them after they split up. They both remarried fairly soon—soon enough that it was apparent they'd both started affairs before their divorce was final.

"After that, the only contact I had with either of them was an occasional note attached to the monthly checks. The checks stopped my senior year in prep school. Since then, the only contact I've had with them is when one of them remarries and wants a wedding present from me."

He sat down again and took one of Sarah's hands in his. "My mother's next husband will be her fourth. Father's still with his second wife, as far as I know."

"Oh, Jake, I'm so sorry." She touched his face with trembling fingers. "But I still don't understand. What have they got to do with us?"

"Don't you see? I can't change my background. All I know about marriage is what I saw when I was a child—a formal kind of bed-hopping. That's not what you want or deserve."

"Of course it isn't. But just because your parents can't get it right doesn't mean you won't. You know there are good marriages. Look at Barbara and Vince, Laura and Colt, Mom and Dad."

"They are part of your heritage, not mine. I can't be like them."

"Yes, you can. You aren't anything like your father and mother. You're not selfish or self-centered. You care about people. And you know a lot about what families need—look at all the things you do for your employees."

"I know families need all the help they can get for even short-term survival. That's all I'm sure of. I love you, Sarah. And you love me. But we can't guarantee it will last. Chances are that sooner or later, one or both of us will fall out of love."

He sat down and hugged her close. "Don't you see? I can't count on you to stay with me forever. My mother didn't stay, and mothers are supposed to love you forever. If my own mother could leave me without a backward glance, then . . ."

"You think I'll leave you, too." Sarah turned her face into his neck. Her heart was breaking. She could see Jake, eight years old, watching his mother walk away from him. How could any woman desert her child? No wonder Jake didn't trust in emotions. He must have spent years training himself not to feel anything at all.

Sarah stiffened. But she wasn't like his mother. She'd never walk away from the man she loved. If he truly loved her, he'd know that.

She pushed out of his arms. "Wait just a darn minute." Jumping up, Sarah stood and stared at the Christmas tree.

"Sarah? What's wrong?"

She held up a hand. "Be quiet." Her emotions were in turmoil, but she had to think clearly. This was important.

A few deep breaths, and she faced him, her hands on her hips. "So this is the problem—I love you and you love me, but we can't get married because you're afraid I'll stop loving you and then I'll leave you. Is that it?"

"Yes. I'm sorry, sweetheart. I can't—"

"You don't trust me to love you forever."

"That's not exactly how I would put it, but—"

"That's the only way to put it. You don't trust me. Therefore, I'm supposed to agree to a tacky affair. A six-month affair."

"I can do without the time limit," Jake said, standing up and reaching for her. "We can stay together as long as it lasts."

Stepping back, Sarah forced herself to ignore the desperation in his voice. "Don't you try to bargain with me, you—you *seducer!* Brannan women don't have affairs. And I wouldn't marry you even if you asked me now, when you're wide-awake. I could never marry a man who didn't trust me."

Jake's eyes turned bleak and hopeless. "I guess that's it, then. Goodbye, Sarah. I'm sorry I wasn't your Mr. Right. I wanted to be. More than anything I've ever wanted before."

Jake walked out the front door.

After the door closed behind him, Sarah sat down and folded her arms around her waist. She stared at the Christmas tree, willing herself to ignore the pain that threatened to tear her apart. Jake couldn't love her, no matter what he'd said. Love was founded in trust, and Jake did not trust her.

After minutes, or hours, she didn't know which, Sarah got up and walked to her bedroom. Taking a suitcase from the top shelf in the closet, she opened it and began packing.

She had to get home. Once she was home again, everything would be all right.

Chapter Ten

Jake stood at the back of the church and waited for one of the ushers to approach him.

"Bride's family or groom's?" the man asked.

"Bride's."

He followed the man down the aisle, past pews draped in white satin. Taking a seat in the second pew from the front, Jake wondered again why he'd felt compelled to come to Boston for his mother's fourth wedding—an elaborate church wedding, no less. He vaguely recalled that her last marriage had been solemnized at a Las Vegas wedding chapel. Somehow, that setting seemed more appropriate for his mother's kind of wedding than the charming ivy-covered church he found himself in this cold February day.

He had no idea why he was here, any more than he'd known why he'd spent Christmas in Vail, skiing, or New Year's in New York. He'd thought Times Square on New Year's Eve was the loneliest place in the world, until he'd returned to Austin and found Sarah's resignation on his desk, along with the completed TimeMaster manual.

Stifling a groan, Jake turned his attention back to the service and studied the woman who'd borne him. She was petite, blond, still beautiful even though she was in her fifties. He was mildly surprised that he felt nothing but pity when he looked at her.

In the past, when he'd seen his mother Jake had been aware of violent emotions—anger, hate, sorrow—bubbling like molten lava beneath the surface of his mind. He'd gotten very good at suppressing those feelings over the years.

Those feelings were gone.

Attending the wedding had served a purpose after all. He'd learned that time had healed his wounds. Time, and Sarah.

How much time would pass before he could think of her and feel nothing at all?

When the ceremony was over and his mother turned to retreat up the aisle, she saw him. She looked startled, but managed a gracious smile as she hurried past his pew.

Later, at the reception, she greeted him with open arms, kissing the air next to his cheek. "Jacob, darling. Why didn't you tell me you were coming?"

"I wasn't sure I'd be able to make it. Business, you know."

Her eyes glittered greedily. "I know. Lawrence, meet my handsome and successful son. You are still successful, aren't you, dear?"

"Yes, mother," he said, shaking hands with the distinguished gray-haired man who was now his stepfather. "Very successful."

Except in matters of the heart. It had taken him years to learn how to fall in love, and he couldn't call his first effort a success. It would probably take him years more to discover how to fall out of love. He'd never be as good at that as his mother was.

She patted him on the shoulder. "I'm so glad. Success is wonderful. Have you heard from your father lately?"

"He called me Christmas morning to thank me for the present I sent him."

"Oh? You exchange Christmas gifts with your father? How quaint." Her voice was cool.

"I brought yours with me." He reached in his pocket and pulled out an envelope. "For Christmas, and for your wedding. Congratulations, mother."

She took the envelope and ripped it open. Apparently there were enough zeros on the check to satisfy her. She smiled, managing to look exactly like a cat who'd just swallowed a tasty mouse. "Thank you, darling." She lifted her cheek for his kiss. "Now, why don't you mingle? There are some lovely women here."

Jake mingled straight out the door of the hotel where the reception was being held. He hailed a taxi and headed to the airport.

When his plane landed in Austin early the next morning, Jake retrieved his car from the parking lot. He didn't go directly home, however.

Instead, he drove around aimlessly for hours, analyzing what was happening to him. Or trying to. Reviewing facts and drawing conclusions from those facts had never been so difficult. Feelings kept intruding, and logic couldn't compete with emotions.

He could think about his mother and he felt sad, in a detached sort of way. After all, he wasn't a lost and lonely little boy anymore. He was old enough to understand exactly why he pitied her—she'd never be satisfied with what she had, because she'd never known what she wanted.

Jake had figured out a long time ago that his mother was always searching for something. When he'd been a little boy, he'd tried very hard to be whatever it was she looked for. For years, he'd strived to be everything she could want in a son.

Jake had thought if he was a good enough son, she'd be a better mother. At the church, he'd finally accepted that no matter what he did, it would never be enough for her, but that wasn't important any longer.

His mother was a selfish, shallow, silly woman.

And Sarah wasn't anything like her.

Jake stifled a groan. He didn't want to think about Sarah, but he couldn't help himself. Memories flashed through his mind's eye.

He remembered how hard he'd worked to convince Sarah to work for him. He'd known from the first that she would be important to him.

He remembered listening to her stories about her life and her family. She might as well have been speaking a foreign language, her stories had been so incomprehensible to him. But her tales had warmed his heart and made him dream sweet dreams again.

He remembered the first time he'd kissed her, the first time she'd confessed that she loved him. He groaned when he remembered that he'd answered her confession with a proposition. She should have given up on him then, but she hadn't. She'd tried to show him what love meant, what families were really about.

She'd invited him to meet the Brannans. She'd taken care of him when he'd been sick.

Grinning involuntarily, Jake remembered Sarah in her outrageous bikini.

She'd also tried to drive him crazy, playing those Brannan woman's games. He remembered Vince and Colt warning him about what to expect. Predicting the tricks she'd pull. Even forearmed, he'd reacted the way she'd wanted him to. He'd been alternately infuriated and flattered, on top of the world when he hadn't been off-balance and out of control. She'd made him fall in love with her. With silly, feminine tricks. With a heart as big as Texas, filled with love for him.

And he'd walked away from that.

He was a fool.

Jake arrived at his condominium and pulled the Jaguar into the darkened garage.

He sat in the car, in the dark, trying to solve the problem of Sarah. This was a situation that could not be solved with logic, or rules, and certainly not by playing games. This was too important to be a game. It was the rest of his life. He could live it alone and scared, or he could trust his gut and his heart and live with Sarah until death did them part.

Jake backed his car out of the garage and drove to Sarah's apartment. When he got to her address, Sarah's red Toyota wasn't parked in front of her apartment. It had been replaced by a black pickup truck.

Jake got out of the car and walked to the front door. He knocked. Rusty Hansen opened the door.

"Where's Sarah?"

Rusty hit him with his fist, the blow catching his left cheekbone.

"Owww!" Jake staggered back, and would have fallen to the ground had Rusty not grabbed his shirt-front and yanked him upright. He pulled back his fist again.

Jake blocked the second blow with his forearm. "Stop! I don't want to fight with you."

"Tough," growled Rusty, trying a left uppercut.

Jake ducked, then moved in close. Using both arms, he shoved as hard as he could against Rusty's stomach. "Tell me where Sarah is, then you can hit me all you want to."

Rusty staggered back a step. "You broke her heart," he grunted.

"I know. I want to fix it. I love her."

Grabbing him by the lapels again, Rusty jerked him close. "And?"

"I want to marry her."

"And?"

"And stay married forever."

Rusty let him go. "About time you realized that. Sarah went home, weeks ago. This is my apartment now."

"Have you seen her? How is she?"

Crossing his arms over his chest, Rusty stared balefully at Jake. "I told you—she's brokenhearted. You want me to spell it out for you?"

Jake shook his head, a lump in his throat.

"Her whole family has you on their list. You'll have to do some fancy talking to get by the Brannans."

"I'm not much of a talker, but I'll do whatever I have to do."

Jake went home, showered and changed into jeans and a sweater. He picked up his razor, then put it back down. Not a good idea. He needed every advantage he could muster and Sarah thought he looked sexy with a day's growth of beard.

He arrived at the Brannan house around ten o'clock that morning. Sarah's car was parked in the driveway. He pulled in behind the Toyota, and got out of his car. Jake walked to the front door and rang the doorbell.

No one answered. He started to turn when a slight movement at the window caught his eye. Someone was home. Whoever it was watched him through the lace curtains.

He pounded on the door. "Let me in. I need to see Sarah." The curtain twitched. A few seconds later, the door opened.

A stranger stood in the doorway. A small female with smooth translucent skin, shrewd blue eyes and snow-white hair. She looked him up and down. "You must be that Logan fellow. Go away."

"Granny Brannan? I thought you were dead."

"Then you're more of an idiot than I was led to believe. Land o' Goshen, do I look dead? I'm alive and kicking and I ought to kick you in the... but it looks like somebody beat me to it." She poked him in the ribs, hard enough to make him wince. "Brannan women don't marry men who are all show and no stay. They marry men who know how to trust, and how to love. You don't."

She slammed the door in his face.

Panicked, Jake beat on the door again. "I can learn! I have learned!"

The door stayed closed.

He waited in front of the house for hours. No one came. No one left. He thought he saw a shadow at a window a few times, but he couldn't be sure.

Jake rubbed the stubble on his chin. God, he was tired. He hadn't slept on the red-eye flight from Boston. He glanced at his watch. He'd been awake twenty-four hours straight and he needed sleep. After he'd slept, he'd be able to figure out what to do. He started the car and backed out. He'd waited long enough. It was time to go back to Austin and regroup.

Sarah pushed the lace curtain aside. "He's leaving! Granny, he's leaving," she wailed.

Her grandmother joined her at the window. "So he is. Are you going to spend all day watching his dust? We have things to do, young lady."

Sarah swallowed the lump in her throat and turned away from the window. "Like what? Not work at the store again. I've been there every day since Christmas. Mom and Dad don't really need our help."

"Yes, they do. And you need to stay busy. Idle hands are the devil's workshop, don't forget. Until you get another job, you'll work at the Brannan Country Store."

"Yes, Granny," Sarah said meekly. She didn't have the energy to argue.

Granny glanced at Sarah and shook her head. "Look at you—you're wasting away, girl. A few more weeks and you'll be nothing but skin and bones. I should have come home before Christmas. If I'd been here, you wouldn't be in this condition. You messed things up with a vengeance, Sarah."

"Me? Me? I didn't set out to break my own heart. If there's a mess around here, I didn't make it. Jake Logan did."

"I know that. But show some spunk, girl. Get over it. A man like him doesn't deserve a Brannan woman.

No man does who doesn't know how to love. You're better off without him."

"I don't think so, Granny. And what if I never get over him? He's everything I ever wanted." Sarah had caught a glimpse of Jake's unshaved, bruised face in the mirror opposite the front door. "Sexy, too." She sighed wistfully. "Even all beat-up like he was."

"I'll give you that. How did you know he had a shiner? You were cowering behind the door."

Sarah straightened her slumping shoulders. "I was not cowering. I just didn't want him to see me."

"I should hope not. Never let a man see you've been crying over him."

"I thought you said a Brannan woman's tears could melt a heart of stone."

"That boy doesn't have a heart."

"He does, too," Sarah snapped. At her grandmother's raised eyebrows, she hastily added, "Honest, Granny. Jake's got a big heart. He just hasn't had much experience using it to love someone. But he could learn, don't you think? With a little help..."

"You're singing a different tune today. Why is that?"

"I don't know what you mean."

Granny snorted. "Oh, yes you do. You're defending that man, after all he put you through. Asking you to marry him, and then having the gall to deny it."

"But he came after me—"

"He didn't rush, did he? It's been weeks since you left him behind." Granny Brannan put her hands on her hips and shook her head. "I should have been here," she repeated. "You needed my advice."

"I had your advice, secondhand from Laura and Barbara."

"Each man is different. Land sakes, child. You can't use the same tricks every time."

"I'm through with tricks. No more games for me." Sarah's shoulders drooped again. "I never was any good at games, anyway."

"That's true. You never were. But you're good at loving, and that boy needs a heap of loving. Maybe he's finally realized that. Like you said, he did come after you."

"Yes, that was a good sign, wasn't it?" Sarah smiled tremulously. "But he left again. Do you think he'll come back?"

Granny shrugged. "Maybe. Maybe not. But even if he does come back, will anything be different? Wedding bells may still put him in a tizzy. Why is he so scared of getting hitched? Answer me that."

"I told you, Granny. His parents—his mother, anyway—marry someone new every week or so. He thinks he's inherited a bad-marriage gene or something."

"That's not it. This Logan fellow is smart as a whip, you said. He knows some marriages last, and some don't." Sarah's grandmother gave her a shrewd look. "What is he so afraid of?"

"He doesn't want to hurt me."

"He's already hurt you. When push comes to shove, most people are more afraid of getting hurt than hurting someone else. Now, you pull yourself together and get to the store. No more moping around today."

Sarah walked to the window and pushed the curtain aside. "He didn't stay long, did he?" she asked mournfully.

Granny Brannan snorted. "Long as his bladder would let him, I reckon."

Jake drove south out of Hamilton, his mind an unanalytical jumble of ideas. When he got to the cutoff to Austin, he didn't take it. Some instinct told him to stay on the highway to San Antonio, instead. He needed help. A friend in the enemy camp, so to speak. Colt McCauley owed him a favor, and he was going to collect.

Two hours later, when he got to San Antonio, he started to go to Colt's office, then remembered it was Saturday. After one stop at a department store downtown, Jake headed for the McCauley house. Ricky—or was it Nicky?—opened the door. Whichever twin it was, he wasn't put off by Jake's disreputable appearance.

"Hi! Wanna play Nintendo?"

"Not today, sport. I'm sort of off games for now. Is your dad at home?"

"Yeah. Who hit you?"

"A real big guy. I need to see your father."

At that moment, Colt appeared at the door. "Go play with your brother," he said to the boy. When the child had scampered up the stairs, he stood back and opened the door wider. "Come right in, Logan."

With a sigh of relief, Jake followed Colt into the house. At least he hadn't slammed the door in his face.

Colt slammed his fist there instead. Jake bounced off the wall and grabbed his right eye. "Owww! Why did you do that?"

"Because you asked for it. We all had a rotten Christmas because of you. Sarah spent the whole day crying her eyes out. She'd counted on a Christmas wedding, you know."

"She cried? Because of me?" Jake grabbed Colt by the shoulders and shook him. "You've got to help me. I've got to see her!"

Colt shrugged Jake's hands off his shoulders. "She's not here. Go to Hamilton."

"I was there, for hours. That white-haired dragon guarding the door wouldn't let me near her."

"Oh, you met Granny Brannan." Colt chuckled, then sobered immediately. "What do you want to see Sarah for?"

"To tell her I love her. To ask her to marry me. Soon. I can't take much more of this. Have you got an ice pack?"

"I don't know. Who else hit you? Vince?"

"Rusty Hansen."

"He did a good job. Your left eye's almost swollen shut."

"I know that. That's why I want an ice bag. I'd like to be able to see out of one eye when I propose."

"Come on. I'll take you to the kitchen and let Laura fix you up. She's real good with bumps and bruises."

Laura took one look and stuck her nose up in the air. "What is that man doing in our house?"

"He wants to marry Sarah. Do we have an ice bag?"

"Yes, but I'm not using it on a man who made my little sister cry. And if you help him, Colt McCauley, I'll never speak to you again. We are not harboring the enemy!"

Jake winced. "I don't want to cause trouble between you two. I'm sorry I ruined your Christmas—I never meant to make Sarah cry."

"Don't worry about it. One good cry is all you were worth. After that, Sarah got over you in two shakes of a lamb's tail."

"No! I don't want her to get over me. I love Sarah!"

"Where do we keep the ice bag?" asked Colt, opening cabinets and drawers. "Aha! Found it." He went to the refrigerator and filled the bag with ice. Handing it to Jake, he told Laura, "Jake is ready to propose. I think he really means it this time."

"So you want to propose, hmm?"

He held the bag to his eye and nodded.

"You already did that once," Laura said. "Then you backed out. How do we know you won't do that again?"

"I'll marry her today."

"Not possible." Colt brought him a glass of water and two aspirin. "You have to have blood tests, get a license—three days minimum."

"Sarah wanted a Christmas wedding," Laura said accusingly. "I know. I'm sorry. But she said Valentine's Day would be good, too. That's Saturday—three days away."

"Christmas, Valentine's Day. What's the difference, Laura?" Colt coaxed. "Either way, they'd never forget their wedding anniversary."

"Whereas a certain day in June is eminently forgettable," said Laura dryly. She rested her chin on her hands and stared at Jake.

He did his best to look the way he felt—contrite and sincere. Whatever she saw must have convinced her of his sincerity.

"We're going to Hamilton this weekend for Granny Brannan's seventy-fifth birthday party Sunday. We haven't seen her since she got back from Paris. I guess we could take you along."

"Paris, Texas?" asked Jake.

"Paris, France. One of our cousins lives there. Rosalie Brannan."

"The model?"

"That's her," said Colt. "The Brannan babe."

Laura made a face at her husband, then returned her attention to Jake. "Well, do you want to go with us?"

Jake nodded. "I sure do."

"We'll have to take a preacher along, too, if you want to get by Granny Brannan."

"Can we do that? What about the license and blood tests?"

"I can get the license. I'll use Laura as a proxy. You get your blood test today, and we'll figure out a way to get Sarah to the doctor for hers. You'd better get a ring, too. Two rings, one for her and one for you. Brannan women like to brand their men."

Jake reached in his jeans' pocket and pulled out a small velvet box. "I already thought of that. I stopped at the first jewelry store I saw after I got to San Antonio." He opened the box. "What do you think."

Laura came closer. She looked at the diamond solitaire and the matching gold bands and nodded. "I'll call Barbara and tell her to start on the wedding cake. I'd better call Mom, too. She can get Granny Brannan's wedding dress out of the attic and send it to the cleaners. Sarah and Granny are about the same size. Daddy plays golf with Reverend Martin every Thursday—he can tell him we need him at the house on Valentine's Day. Can you think of anything else, Colt?"

"Not a thing, honey. Oh, I'll call Vince and Rusty and tell them to get their tuxes out of mothballs."

"Please do. We don't want them smelling up the house like they stunk up the church at our wedding." Laura gave Jake a questioning look.

"It all sounds fine to me." He'd lost control. Somehow, it didn't bother him. Having family rally round to help him out felt good. But they were more sure of Sarah's response than he was. "But aren't we taking a lot for granted? What if she turns me down? Maybe I should call her now and tell her—"

Laura shook her head. "Not a good idea. She won't believe you mean it. Not unless you're right there in front of her, ready to go through with it." She gave him the first genuine smile he'd seen from her all day. "Besides, I like the idea of a surprise wedding. We've never had one of those before."

Chapter Eleven

Sarah woke up early Saturday morning. Her first thought was of Jake Logan. He'd been her first thought every morning, and her last thought every night for weeks, and it had to stop. She had to find a way to forget him.

He hadn't come back. It had been three whole days since he'd knocked on the front door, and he had not returned. She had to accept the truth.

Jake Logan was never coming back.

She swallowed a sob. She was not going to cry one more tear for him, not one. He wasn't worth it, and besides, if she let one more tear fall, Granny Brannan would be all over her like a duck on a June bug. She thought Sarah was making herself sick over Jake—she'd insisted that Sarah go to the doctor for a blood test. Granny Brannan absolutely refused to let her talk about him.

Granny's lack of compassion wasn't the only thing that was wrong. The whole family was acting strangely.

Mysterious telephone calls, conversations that stopped when she entered the room, trips to the attic in the middle of the night—she'd heard the footsteps overhead—and, to top it off, suddenly she wasn't getting any sympathy at all.

Sarah put on a robe and wandered into the kitchen. The coffee was perking, so she wasn't the first one up. Granny Brannan came in, carrying a large, wrapped box. "Here you are. Open this."

"A present for me? Why? It's your birthday, not mine." She kissed Granny Brannan on the cheek. "Happy birthday."

"Don't rush your fences. My birthday's not until tomorrow. This is a Valentine's Day present," Granny said gruffly. "Now take this, open it and put it on. And do something about your hair. It looks like a rat's nest."

"Gee, thanks, Granny. What's going on? You never gave me a Valentine's present before."

"You never looked like death warmed over before. Think of it as a bribe. I don't want you ruining my birthday celebration tomorrow. You put on what's in that box, and fix yourself up. No matter how bad you feel, you're going to act cheerful this weekend if it kills you." She put the box in her hands and shoved her down the hall. "Go on, now."

Sarah took the package to her room and opened it. She found a beautiful rose-colored dress, with white lace at the collar and cuffs. She held it up to her, and looked in the mirror. What would Jake think if he saw her in a dress like this, she wondered, a dress with a high collar and a sassy full skirt that skimmed the tops of her knees?

She almost cried when she realized she was thinking about Jake again, but Granny's orders echoed in her mind. Granny Brannan was right, as usual. She couldn't spoil her birthday.

With one last shuddering sigh, Sarah squared her shoulders and did as she was told. When she was showered, shampooed, madeup and wearing her new dress, she returned to the kitchen. No one was there.

Her mother and grandmother were in the family room rearranging furniture. Nora looked up and smiled at her. "What a pretty dress."

"It's a present from Granny Brannan. Thank you, Granny. That couch looks heavy. Do you need any help?"

"No, we're almost done. We wanted to make room for the crowd that's coming. Tomorrow." Sarah's mother smiled again and Sarah thought her smile looked a little misty.

"You look lovely, Sarah. That dress needs something, though. I know just the thing." Granny Brannan went to a cabinet in the corner of the room and retrieved the carved wooden box where she kept her treasures. "Wear this." She took out a gold filigree lavaliere with a heart-shaped locket hanging from it. "I wore it when your grandfather asked me to marry him."

Sarah's eyes filled with tears. "Th-thank you, Granny. It's lovely."

Granny Brannan fastened the old-fashioned necklace around Sarah's neck. "There, now you're ready."

"Ready for what?"

"Valentine's Day, of course. What else?"

Sarah frowned. "Isn't it a little early? And we don't usually make a big to-do over Valentine's Day—not when we always have a party for you the day after."

"Well, we should. Valentine's Day is important, too. Just as important as my birthday, in fact."

"Yes," agreed Sarah's mother. "We need some new traditions. So we're going to have a special Valentine's Day celebration—the first of many."

"Does everyone know about this but me?"

Granny Brannan and Nora exchanged guilty glances.

"Oh, I get it. You didn't tell me until this morning because I've been such a mope. Well, I promise I'll be cheerful. Just because today is the day for lovers and—"

"I think I hear a car in the driveway," said Granny. "I bet the San Antonio contingent is arriving now."

Sure enough, the twins came bursting through the door, followed by Colt and Laura, both heavily laden with packages. They had not come alone.

Jake Logan stood in the doorway, his eyes hidden behind dark glasses. "Hello, Sarah."

"What are you doing here?" She couldn't take her eyes off him. He looked wonderful. "Laura, Colt? Did you bring him?"

She tore her gaze from Jake and looked around. Colt, Laura, the twins, her mother and Granny Brannan had disappeared. She was alone with Jake Logan.

"Sarah—"

She backed away from him. "Go away. I don't want to see you."

"Too bad. You're going to see me every day for the rest of our lives." He followed her, until her back was against the kitchen counter. "Sarah, I love you."

"Jake, I'm warning you. You can't love someone you don't trust. If you say that one more time, I'm going to hit you."

He took off his glasses. "Go ahead, I'm getting used to it. Anywhere but the eyes, okay?" He crowded closer. "I love you, Sarah."

Sarah touched the side of his face with trembling fingers. "Does it hurt?" she whispered, her heart swelling with love.

"Like hell."

She snatched her hand back. "Good. I want you to hurt. A lot." Sarah wasn't about to let him off easy. The man had broken her heart, for heaven's sake. Just because her heart was beating a happy rhythm now didn't mean Jake was home free.

"You Brannan women have a mean streak, you know that?"

Sarah gasped indignantly. "That's not true! Brannan women are the kindest, gentlest, sweetest women in the world. Ask any man who married one."

"I don't have to ask. I know that." He went down on one knee. Taking her hand in his, he squinted up at her through his colorfully bruised eyes. "Sarah Jane Brannan, will you please marry me?"

She pinched his wrist.

"Ouch. Why did you do that?"

"I wanted to see if you were awake. Are you?"

"Wide-awake. Please marry me."

"No. When? Next month? Next year? You'll change your mind. I know you will. You'll decide I'm not dependable, and you'll convince yourself I'm going to leave you, so you'll leave me first. For all I know, you'll leave me at the altar."

"No, I won't. I'll never leave you. And you'll never leave me. And there won't be any altar. We're getting married right here. Today. It's all arranged."

"What do you mean, it's all arranged. I haven't said yes."

"You will. Laura said you would. So did your mother and your grandmother. Barbara, too. I took a poll."

"A poll?"

"A very unscientific poll, I'm afraid. But I had to, Sarah. I was scared you might say no. But all the Brannan women assured me you'd say yes." Jake fumbled in his pocket. "Look, I have the rings, see?"

She barely glanced at them. "Weddings take time to plan. We can't get married today."

"Yes, we can. Colt helped me get the license. We've had the blood tests, too. And Reverend Martin will be here any minute."

"I didn't have a blood—oh, yes, I did. So that's why Granny Brannan made me go to the doctor. Does my whole family know what's going on?"

"Yes. And they've all helped us get ready for it. Barbara baked a wedding cake, and Granny Brannan is going to loan you her wedding dress. So you have to say yes. Soon. You've got to change dresses. Please. I love you, Sarah. I trust you, too."

Sarah didn't know whether to laugh or cry, so she did a little of both. She took Jake by the hand and tugged him to his feet. "I know that. I love you, too. But how long do you think I'll stick around?"

"Forever."

"I thought you didn't believe in forever."

"I do now. Besides, even if you wanted to, the Brannan family would never let you leave me."

Sarah gave him a brilliant smile. "That's true. They wouldn't let you get away from me, either."

"Does that mean you'll marry me?"

"Yes."

Jake gave a yell, took her in his arms and swung her around. The kitchen was suddenly filled with Brannans, hugging and kissing and carrying on.

Sarah's husband hunt had come to an end. Another Brannan woman had got her man.

* * * * *

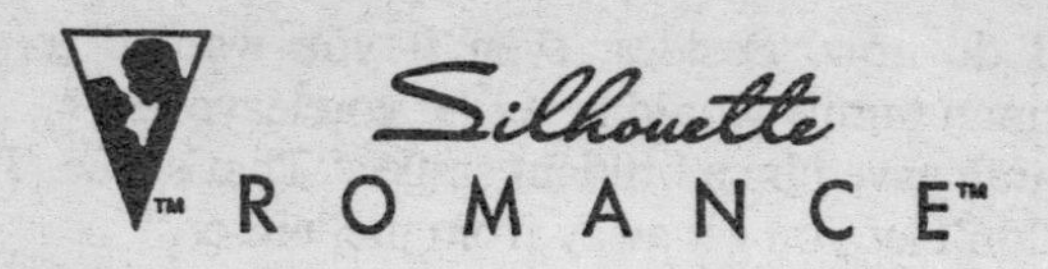

COMING NEXT MONTH

#1138 A FATHER FOR ALWAYS—Sandra Steffen
Fabulous Fathers
To keep his daughter, single dad Jace McCall needed a fake fiancée—fast! So when he asked Garret Fletcher to be his preter bride, Garret couldn't refuse. After all, she didn't have to preten she was in love....

#1139 INSTANT MOMMY—Annette Broadrick
Daughters of Texas/Bundles of Joy
Widowed dad Deke Crandal knew horses and cattle—not newbo baby girls! So how could Mollie O'Brien resist Deke's request fo help? Especially when she secretly wished to be a permanent par of the family.

#1140 WANTED: WIFE—Stella Bagwell
Lucas Lowrimore was ready to settle down—with Miss Right. H just didn't expect to fall for pretty police officer Jenny Prescott. She was definitely the wife he wanted, but Jenny proved to be a hard woman to win!

#1141 DEPUTY DADDY—Carla Cassidy
The Baker Brood
Carolyn Baker had to save her orphaned godchildren from their uncle, Beau Randolf! What would a single farmer know about *tw* infants? But Beau wasn't the greenhorn Carolyn had expected!

#1142 ALMOST MARRIED—Carol Grace
Laurie Clayton thought she'd never love again—until Cooper Buckingham charmed her and the baby she was caring f Everything seemed perfect when they were together, almost as i they were married! But would Laurie ever be able to take a chan and say, "I do"?

#1143 THE GROOM WORE BLUE SUEDE SHOES—Jessica Travis
With his sensuous sneer and bedroom eyes, Travor Steele was a dead ringer for Elvis Presley. But it was gonna take a whole lott shakin' to convince Erin Weller that he wasn't the new king—b her next groom!

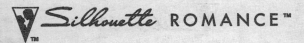